"You're going to tell me the whole story," Sophia said.

He'd never been a fan of her using his general's tone, but if any situation required it, this was the one.

"I am," Frank replied, with both hands on the steering wheel once more. "You're not going to like it."

"I already don't like it, Frank."

"The man following you was one of the top snipers in the Afghanistan military. One word from his boss and your life is over."

She sucked in a breath. "Why?" Who would make her a target?

"That's one detail. I swear to you, as soon as I'm sure we're out of harm's way, I'll tell you everything."

"Harm's way or not, you'll tell me everything tonight." He wasn't the only one who could issue orders.

With a short nod, he rolled his broad shoulders.

She remembered the feel of those shoulders under her hands after a tough day at work when she'd help him work out the kinks...or late at night in the heat of passion.

Oh, how she wanted to trust him, to be sure she could trust him.

It scared her, more than being run off the road, just how much she wanted to believe in Frank Leone again.

HEAVY ARTILLERY HUSBAND

USA TODAY Bestselling Authors

DEBRA WEBB & REGAN BLACK

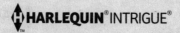
HARLEQUIN® INTRIGUE®

Recycling programs
for this product may
not exist in your area.

ISBN-13: 978-0-373-74953-9

Heavy Artillery Husband

Copyright © 2016 by Debra Webb

Printed in U.S.A.

www.Harlequin.com

Debra Webb, born in Alabama, wrote her first story at age nine and her first romance at thirteen. It wasn't until she spent three years working for the military behind the Iron Curtain—and a five-year stint with NASA—that she realized her true calling. Since then the *USA TODAY* bestselling author has penned more than one hundred novels, including her internationally bestselling Colby Agency series.

Regan Black, a *USA TODAY* bestselling author, writes award-winning, action-packed novels featuring kick-butt heroines and the sexy heroes who fall in love with them. Raised in the Midwest and California, she and her family, along with their adopted greyhound, two arrogant cats and a quirky finch, reside in the South Carolina Lowcountry, where the rich blend of legend, romance and history fuels her imagination.

Books by Debra Webb and Regan Black

Harlequin Intrigue

Colby Agency: Family Secrets

Gunning for the Groom
Heavy Artillery Husband

The Specialists: Heroes Next Door

The Hunk Next Door
Heart of a Hero
To Honor and To Protect
Her Undercover Defender

Visit the Author Profile page at
Harlequin.com for more titles.

CAST OF CHARACTERS

Sophia Leone—Former military analyst and widow of brigadier general Frank Leone, she is the founder of Leo Solutions, a security company she and her husband dreamed of establishing after he retired.

Frank Leone—Nearing the end of his army career, he accepted an undercover assignment that made progress until it spiraled out of control. Now presumed dead, Frank is trying to protect his wife and daughter from a criminal group out for vengeance.

Kelly Halloran—A retired army general and friend of the Leones, he seized an opportunity few men would have the audacity to pursue. Now he sits at the pinnacle of a highly skilled and highly profitable operation.

Victoria Colby-Camp—The semiretired head of the Colby Agency. She and her husband, Lucas Camp, can't seem to stay out of the business of investigations.

Chapter One

Chicago, Illinois
Monday, April 18, 6:45 p.m.

Sophia Leone sat back as the waiter delivered wide shallow bowls filled with the best pasta in the Windy City. From the first warm embrace upon her arrival, her friend Victoria Colby-Camp and her husband, Lucas Camp, had carefully kept the conversation on lighthearted topics.

It couldn't stay that way. All three of them recognized there were serious matters to address. As the founder of the Colby Agency, Victoria never let her mind stray too far from business, especially not when she sensed a friend in trouble.

Was she in trouble? Sophia couldn't decide. She was still processing everything that had happened over the past few days.

She resisted the urge to run her fingers over the fading goose egg on her scalp. Hidden by her hair just above her ear, it was the only remnant of the shocking fight in her kitchen. Though it had been a terrible ordeal, the real culprit was in custody and the people who mattered most were safe. Coming to Chicago gave her a chance to escape and some space to decide how she wanted to move forward.

While this visit to Chicago needed to shift into business, tonight was for pleasure. She wanted time to relax and catch up with her friends. She hadn't realized just how pervasive that undercurrent of tension in her life had been during the months when her daughter, Frankie, refused to speak with her. Now it was marvelous to share how happily Frankie and her fiancé, Aidan, a former Colby Agency investigator, were coming along with their wedding plans. With countless questions and decisions remaining, the two most important details were finalized. They'd set a date for September and Aidan's family would be in attendance.

"I'm still not sure we've forgiven you for stealing Aidan away," Lucas teased when the waiter walked away. "Victoria had to get creative when she recruited him."

"He was ready to try this side of the pond."

Victoria shot her husband an amused glance. "I might've implied that when the river turned green on St. Patrick's Day, Chicago would feel like Ireland."

Watching the banter between the pair made Sophia's heart twist painfully. It reminded her so much of the wonderful days when she'd felt that camaraderie and partnership with her own husband. Brigadier General Franklin Leone had been dead almost a year now and she still couldn't quite accept it.

She took a bite of her meal and worked hard to enjoy the fresh flavors of tender pasta and crisp vegetables. She would not let a wave of loneliness ruin the evening. Doing her best to keep up her end of the conversation, she shared more about her future son-in-law. "Aidan is mesmerized with the Seattle area. He hasn't seen much beyond the sights downtown, but when they dropped me at the airport this morning, he and Frankie were planning a visit to Tillicum Village this weekend. It's a traditional native tribal experience."

"I remember making that trip ages ago," Lucas said. "They'll have a fantastic time."

"You know, I think he might be considering it for the rehearsal dinner." Sophia smiled with anticipation. "It would be quite memorable if it works out."

Victoria's eyes sparkled. "Their wedding will be memorable, regardless. I know we're both looking forward to attending."

"And Frankie can't wait to have you both join us," Sophia replied. With so much to celebrate, it was silly of her to dwell on who *wouldn't* be there. She took another bite of her pasta, washed it down with a sip of excellent wine and struggled again to forgive her husband for missing this incredible milestone in their daughter's life.

Victoria leaned forward and lowered her voice. "If everything is perfect and wonderful, why are you only poking at your dinner?"

Sophia lifted her gaze and met the concern shining in her friend's eyes. Victoria was as sharp as any of the private investigators she kept on her staff. While all three of them knew this dinner was meant to be comforting, neither she nor Victoria had ever been good at beating around the proverbial bush.

Sophia smiled. "I just can't say thank you enough." Without Victoria, she and her daughter might never have been reconciled.

Victoria set her fork aside and reached for her glass of wine. "You've said thank you more than enough already—none of which was necessary. I'm happy for you and Frankie, even if it cost me a top investigator."

Why had Sophia come all this way if she wasn't going to be honest about her other concerns? This wasn't something to discuss over a phone or a video chat later. She wanted to see their immediate reactions when she asked her questions. Sophia tried to muster some courage. Shy and uncertain weren't typical for her. She was accustomed to boldly heading exactly where she needed to go in a conversation or in business.

"Aidan is remarkable," Sophia said with a tight smile. "You should see them together." Here she went again, dancing around the more pertinent issue. *Get to the point!*

"We'll see them at the wedding." Victoria's smile didn't quite ease the curiosity in her eyes. "But I'm sure that's not why you've come all this way, Sophia."

"Should I excuse myself?" Lucas asked.

"Of course not," Sophia replied immediately. Whatever she told Victoria would find its way to Lucas anyway. She didn't begrudge them that. It had been the same in her own marriage. Until those last two years anyway, when his overseas operations put more than geography obstacles between her and her husband.

Why couldn't she just get the words out? It wasn't as if Victoria wouldn't understand her predicament. By now her friend had probably guessed why she'd made the trip. "You know I still have questions about Frank."

Both Lucas and Victoria nodded, though neither offered any comment.

Her husband had been found guilty of treason during his last deployment. Before he could be transferred to prison, he'd killed himself, leaving Frankie and Sophia to deal with the fallout. When she closed her eyes at night, the memory of watching that closed-circuit monitor fill with the image of his pale, lifeless face haunted her. Sophia suspected he had carried terrible secrets to his grave. Secrets that might not even have answers.

Though Frankie believed her father was innocent of the treason charge and was certain he'd been murdered, there had never been a scrap of evidence to support her theory. It was only one facet of the complex situation that had wedged them apart.

While Sophia had accepted she'd always be curious about her husband's last days, it was her internal battle that had brought her to Chicago. During her career as a military analyst, she'd taken information and made concise assessments. Now she wondered if her ability to read people and situations had failed her.

"Not just Frank." Sophia shook her head.

"It's Paul, too." In the wake of Frank's suicide, she'd needed to act quickly to protect her future and Frankie's, as well. Paul Sterling, an old friend, had helped her launch Leo Solutions, the security company she and her husband had envisioned to keep them busy after his retirement. Mere days ago she'd found out Paul had betrayed her in favor of his own interests.

How had she allowed two men to fool her so completely?

"Every way I look at what's happened," Sophia went on, "the common denominator is my judgment or lack thereof." She picked up her fork, stabbing a stem of roasted asparagus and dragging it through the light cream sauce. "Forget I said anything." She glanced from Victoria to Lucas. "I don't really know what I need, or even what I want to do next. Please, let's talk about something else."

"All right," Victoria said. "Have you found your dress for the wedding?"

"I have something in mind." Sophia felt her smile bloom. It happened whenever she toyed with ideas for the upcoming wedding. While the final choices would be up to Frankie and Aidan, she loved window-shopping and perusing magazines and online sites for creative ideas to present to the bride and groom.

"It's all happened so quickly, I've only been shopping online so far. Frankie hasn't had any time to decide on colors or venues, though she made me promise not to wear something that fades into the decor. I thought I might shop a bit while I'm here."

"We should go together," Victoria said with an eager smile. "The mother of the bride should dazzle, but not quite as much as the bride herself. Has Frankie given any thought to her dress?"

"Not particularly. You know she wasn't the type of little girl who played wedding day dress up like so many of her friends." Sophia curled her fingers around the hemmed edge of the napkin in her lap, assaulted by memories of happier times. "I don't want to jinx it, but I'm hoping she'll choose to have my wedding gown altered and restyled to make it hers."

"Oh, that would be beautiful." Victoria blinked rapidly. "You're all right with the idea?"

"I suggested it." Sophia forgot to take the bite of pasta she'd gathered onto her fork. "She loves the traditional, understated lines of my wedding dress and it's a way for her to include her father." Sophia felt bittersweet tears at the back of her throat. She would not cry another tear for Frank or his memory. "She wants to honor the start of our family as she starts her own."

"Sounds as though your daughter's a thoughtful and compassionate young woman," Lucas said.

Sophia could have hugged him. It was the perfect assessment and a lovely way to put it. "Thank you. I think so, too."

Her gaze dropped to her plate as her mind drifted back to that idyllic time when the future was a bright, hope-filled horizon. The Leone family had faced the world together as a team. She'd weathered the highs and lows with her husband during his military career. Just when they were on the cusp of the next stage—ready to enjoy their empty nest and launch a new venture—life had fallen to pieces. Countless times over the past year, she'd fought off the urge to scream and wave her fist at that deceptive horizon. *Life is not always fair, Sophia.*

"Frankie still believes he was innocent, doesn't she?" Lucas asked.

Sophia nodded, her heart heavy. "Her faith in him is relentless and even stronger now since Paul revealed his true colors."

"She's Frank's daughter through and through," Victoria observed. "I saw it the moment she walked into my office. She has his stride, his chin and all of his tenacity."

"Among other things," Sophia admitted. There were moments, such as this one, when the sadness at the scope of her loss flattened her. She tossed her napkin over the remainder of her dinner and swallowed back another wave of unanswerable questions. Her fingers locked in her lap and she squeezed until her knuckles protested.

Victoria leaned forward, her voice low. "Keeping your worries bottled up isn't helping you move forward."

"If you'd rather discuss what's troubling you elsewhere, we can wrap this up," Lucas offered.

"That's kind of you both, but not necessary. I'm overthinking things." Sophia tried to believe that explanation as she unclenched her hands, automatically rubbing the place where her wedding rings had been. She'd taken them off the day after the funeral, when any reminder of her ties to her disgraced husband would impede the launch of Leo Solutions. As a family, they'd been so close. As a couple, they'd focused their plans on giving Frankie a solid foundation. How had it suddenly crumbled?

"Frankie wasn't the only one to dig into Frank's case. I've been discreet," Sophia confessed. "I haven't found anything helpful or conclusive yet. It would be nice to confirm my suspicions about his guilt or innocence. Frankie views him with a daughter's hero worship. I won't take that away from her."

"Of course not," Victoria agreed.

"After the things Paul said and did last week, it made me wonder about Frank all over again." Sophia recognized that Victoria knew more than her fair share about pain and betrayal. She understood how betrayal often led a person to ignore some details and put more weight on other points, which blurred the facts into something closer to fiction. "Maybe Frankie's right and we should try harder to clear her dad's name."

"Say the word and I'll have one of our investigators start digging into it."

Sophia appreciated Victoria's offer. It came as no surprise, and professional assistance was one more reason to be here in person. She should say yes and let Victoria handle it while she went back to help Frankie with wedding plans. Would the answers change anything? Her husband was dead, a convicted traitor—it wasn't a simple matter at all. The problem was still too sensitive, too fresh even a year after the verdict.

Now that the offer was on the table, she wasn't sure an investigation was the right way to go. "Maybe we should investigate." As the words left her mouth, everything felt all wrong. "Or maybe not." Exasperated with herself, she tried to laugh. "What do I know?"

Her throat tight with frustration, she raised her glass and finished off her wine. Her hotel was just down the street and she didn't have to worry about driving. The bold flavors of the wine melted on her tongue but didn't give her any insight or steady her nerves. Didn't she *want* the answers? Wouldn't that help her sleep at night?

Assuming Victoria's investigators could find the truth, knowing the facts wouldn't actually change anything. Frankie would still be short one outstanding father. As Sophia had reviewed Frank's last few years, even amid all the chaos and inevitable suspicion, she'd never doubted his love or devotion to their daughter.

"Why don't we launch the investigation? You can call it off at any time," Lucas said.

No, it was better not to start at all. "Perhaps," Sophia replied at last, "his secrets, good or bad, are better left buried."

"Even if he was murdered?"

"I know what Frankie believes and I can't blame her. Suicide doesn't fit the Frank Leone we knew and loved." Sophia carried the burden of that heartache in the locked muscles across her shoulders. "I didn't tell her or anyone else how he changed, how he pulled away from me at the end. I'm not sure she ever needs to know about those final months."

Though they hadn't been aware back then that it would be the end. Sophia had thought there would be time for him to come around and be himself once more. She'd talked about it with a therapist, focused on shoring up her weaknesses, never expecting Frank to break.

"You have excellent instincts, Sophia. What do *you* know?" Victoria prompted.

"Certainly my husband had enemies capable of staging a suicide." Though she'd searched, none of his obvious adversaries had been in the area at the time of his death. "Even if by some miracle of detective work we could pinpoint a culprit now, bringing that person to justice would likely be impossible."

"That's a fair point." Lucas nodded sagely. "And it would create a distraction and turmoil when you and Frankie should be focused on happier events."

"Yes," Sophia agreed. "That's exactly the issue. I don't want to do anything that would cast a cloud over her wedding day. She and I might have unanswered, even unanswerable questions, but we're finally at a point where we both feel as though we have strong family ties again." She leaned back as the waiter removed dishes and poured more wine. When he was gone, she admitted, "Part of my hesitation is that I don't want to be proven right, either."

Lucas's brow furrowed. "What do you mean?"

"If the verdict was correct, if Frank did commit treason, I don't want to confirm that and destroy Frankie's fond memories. Whatever happened in his final assignment, he did everything right as a dad."

"We understand completely," Victoria said. "If you change your mind at any time, the offer is there for you."

"Thank you for listening and letting me ramble on about it."

"If you want my professional assessment, I'll say your instincts haven't been compromised in the slightest," Victoria declared in her trademark steely tone. "Paul took advantage while you were distracted by grief, that's all. Whatever Frank didn't tell you about his career or his personal problems, he loved you and Frankie above all else. He must have been protecting you."

"He loved Frankie." During those last two years, Sophia had lost her faith that her husband loved her with equal devotion. He'd grown distant and secretive. She'd tried and failed to chalk it up to his protective nature.

Victoria consulted her watch. "One more minute for self-pity and then I'm ordering an outrageous dessert for all of us to share."

Lucas pretended to protest, shifting his chair close enough to drape an arm across the back of Victoria's.

They looked utterly content as a couple, as a team. Sophia had had that once, for nearly the entirety of her thirty-year marriage. However, that period of her life had ended, and she needed to focus on the good times, to let the uncertainty go.

"I don't need even one more minute." Sophia reached into her purse for her cell phone. "Let me show you some pictures of far more important things."

She brought up a slide show and together the three of them admired the options Frankie would eventually sort out, from bouquets and centerpieces to tuxedo tails and cake flavors. "We've already decided to surprise Aidan with an old family recipe for the groom's cake."

"This will be a dream day for all of you," Victoria said with a wistful smile. "You must be so excited."

"We're going to have so much fun with the planning. Both of them are huge assets to

Leo Solutions. I have so much to look forward to." Catching herself gushing, she paused for a breath. "I thought I'd lost that relationship with her forever. You returned it to me, Victoria. You and Aidan." There weren't enough thank-yous to adequately express her joy that her daughter was healthy, happy and thriving again. It truly was time to stop dwelling on the past and let go of the questions that would never have answers.

Sophia insisted on paying for dinner, managing to win a lighthearted argument with Lucas over the check. As they parted ways at the restaurant door, a shopping date scheduled for tomorrow, she chose to walk rather than accept Victoria's offer for a ride to the hotel. The crisp spring breeze drifting off the lake caught at her hair, boosting her mood as she headed down the street.

Moments after Victoria's car pulled away, she regretted her decision. Without the distraction of conversation, she felt eyes on her immediately. A chill raised the hair at the back of her neck and she called on her years of self-discipline not to show any recognition to her observer. She knew she would be safe enough as long as she was surrounded by other pedestrians.

Though she hadn't made a secret of her

travel plans to Chicago, she couldn't imagine who would bother watching her. Mind over matter, she thought as she put one foot in front of the other, shoulders back, head high, refusing to let her discomfort show.

The tactic had served her well as a general's wife, an analyst and a mother. Opponents large and small had cowered in the face of her poise and determination. Let whoever was out there watch. Let them see Sophia Leone hadn't changed a bit as a widow or under the pressure of the events that followed.

Poised or not, she felt a wave of relief wash over her when she entered the hotel lobby, interrupting that intense, uncomfortable scrutiny. She crossed to the front desk with a smile on her face. She might as well extend her reservation for an additional night. One day of shopping with Victoria might not be enough.

"Ah, Ms. Leone, of course. And you have a message."

"I do?" Sophia was surprised. Frankie would have called her cell.

The man behind the desk passed her a small envelope embossed with the hotel logo. Sophia noted the precise block lettering of her name on the outside. Memories whispered through her, making her shiver. Frank had preferred that style over his nearly illegible cursive handwriting. They'd often joked that he had the penmanship of a doctor. How rude of someone to try to irritate her by mimicking his habit. She caught herself in the middle of the over-reaction. Printed lettering wasn't a personal attack or automatic insult. She chalked up her edginess to having been watched so closely on her brief walk. Moving down the hall toward the elevators, she opened the envelope and pulled out the note.

She quickly read it through. She grabbed at the nearest wall for support as her knees buckled. *You and Frankie are in danger. Meet me at Parkhurst by nine. Prepare to run.*

It wasn't signed, but the writing, the location told her it had to be from Frank. That was impossible. He was dead.

Parkhurst, the US Army Reserve Center just off the old Route 66. She and Frank had been there once for a dining out, early in his career. They'd just learned she was pregnant. She remembered avoiding the wine but not the curious speculation of the other wives. She pressed a hand to her mouth to smother the whimper building in her throat. This wasn't happening. Couldn't be. She needed to get to her room. Needed to return to the desk and get a description of who had delivered the message.

Her stomach tightened while she read the

note again more slowly. The meaning didn't register at all as her fingertip followed the bold swipe of the pen strokes making up each letter and word. Her body sighed with memories of those happier times.

With an effort, she straightened her spine, tucked away the nostalgia and pulled herself together. Whoever had created this note had forged Frank's handwriting perfectly. Sophia swallowed and forced herself to take a deep, calming breath. Frank wasn't the only person in the world to write this way. He wasn't the only person who would choose a remote location for a discreet meeting. At the edge of the nature preserve surrounding the facility, there would be plenty of privacy at night.

She walked back to the front desk, hoping she didn't look as pale as she felt. When the clerk smiled, she held up the note. "Can you tell me who left this and when?"

The young man on duty shook his head. "It was here when I came on an hour ago. Jenny only told me it was urgent, according to the man who left it."

"Man?"

The desk clerk nodded.

She pressed her lips together as potential images and thoughts collided like bumper cars in her head. "Could I access your security footage?"

"Um, no? That kind of thing would have to be approved by our—"

"It's okay," she said, cutting his protest short. What were the odds the person who'd written the missive had had the audacity to deliver it? Zero to none. She tapped the note against her palm. "Thank you for your time."

Shoulders back, she aimed for the elevator once more. Frank was *dead*. She'd seen him in that morgue. Dead men didn't send notes inviting their widowed wives to meetings, advising them to run. Someone was attempting to put her off balance. She hitched her shoulders at the thought of being watched during her walk from the restaurant. Someone wanted to frighten her and lure her from the safety of the hotel.

Defiant, she reached out and punched the call button for the elevator. When the car arrived, she shoved the note into her purse, ignoring it. She would not be influenced by the emotions of her past. It would be foolish to dash out to a relatively deserted area alone. She knew better than to take that sort of risk.

When she reached her room, she found another note on the floor just inside the doorway. Someone had slipped it under the door.

No name on the envelope this time. She tore it open and tears sprang to her eyes as she skimmed it. The message was the same handwriting as the note left at the desk, but the first word stole her breath.

Dolcezza.

Stunned, she went limp and slid to the floor, the wall her only support. Her gaze was locked on the precious endearment Frank had used from their first date through every phone call and letter when they were apart. She pressed her lips together, holding back the wail of frustration and pain swelling in her throat.

So he'd called her sweetheart in Italian. Any number of people might know that detail about their lives. This did not mean Frank had miraculously returned from the dead. Whoever was orchestrating this was pushing all the right buttons, prodding her to make a predictable response. *Melodramatic and cruel*, she thought, checking her watch. If she left now, she'd just get to Parkhurst in time. Options ran through her mind. Victoria could help her sort out who had delivered the message. She could certainly find someone to ride with her or shadow her to the meeting.

But what if it *was* Frank?

What was she thinking? Her husband was

dead, his body buried in Seattle. She thought suddenly about the closed casket. *What if...?*

No. Her husband had been an incredible man and she'd loved him from that first moment through all the ups and downs of marriage and career to the farewell she hadn't known would be their last. She'd stood by him against the treason charges despite her doubts.

She glanced at the note, heard his voice whispering *"dolcezza"* at her ear when she read it again. Absolutely not. Remarkable he might've been, but not even Frank could come back from the dead. Shoving the second note into her purse with the first, she dragged herself from the floor and went to the bathroom to freshen up.

When she came out, the notes taunted her. Her maternal instinct kicked into high gear. While she might ignore a veiled threat against herself, she couldn't leave Frankie's safety to chance. Her daughter had worked tirelessly to triumph over a devastating physical injury and subsequent emotional turmoil. She wouldn't let any vicious stunt ruin things now.

Determination beating urgently in her veins, Sophia packed her overnight bag. She considered changing clothes, but only switched from her heels to her flats. Her lightweight black sweater and slacks were easy to move in and the closest things to camouflage in her wardrobe. Whoever was waiting for her at Parkhurst, she had to go.

Nothing and no one would prevent her from keeping Frankie safe and her future secure.

Chapter Two

Sophia sent her daughter a quick text message while she waited for the valet to bring her rental car from the hotel parking garage. She breathed a sigh of relief at the quick, normal reply. She was sure this meeting was bogus and equally sure she couldn't let it slide. Though she might be heading into the unknown alone, she intended to leave a trail of bread crumbs in case things went wrong. A lesson she'd learned from her husband—anticipate the best while creating a strategy to fend off the worst.

When the car arrived, she loaded her suitcase into the backseat and kept her purse up front. She left her cell phone on and synced it to the car's system. When the navigation software had a route ready for her, she pulled away from the hotel.

Frank wouldn't be there—couldn't possibly be there—but she had yet to come up with a plausible reason why anyone would impersonate him to get her attention.

Darkness fell as she made her way along historic Route 66 and headlights winked on under the purpling sky in her rearview mirror. Having memorized the brief note, she let the cadencc of the words play through her mind over and over. Rubbing a pressure point on her earlobe, she blinked back a sudden rush of tears.

She'd thought the well had run dry months ago. Those early days after Frank killed himself had been wave after wave of sobbing, until she thought she'd never breathe properly again. Throughout their marriage she'd been alone frequently, always with the confident knowledge that she'd see him again. While their daughter bitterly accused her of moving on too quickly in establishing the security business, the harsh, lonely truth of how much she missed Frank had thankfully been buried under a mountain of new career distractions.

A car rushed up behind her and passed her in a blur. She glanced down, confirming she was driving the speed limit, and forgot the other car as it surged into the distance. She had more important things to consider. Who would be waiting for her at Parkhurst and why? How would she handle the encounter?

Maybe she should *call* Frankie and put her

on alert. *You could be in danger* wasn't suitable for a text message. Sophia checked the clock. She could pull over and snap a picture of the notes with her phone and still arrive on time for the meeting.

That sort of move would only send her daughter and, by extension, the upper management of Leo Solutions into a tailspin of worry for Frankie and Sophia. Better to send an update when she had some facts about the situation rather than encourage useless conjecture that might stir up more trouble. Maintaining a good reputation within the industry of security services meant mitigating bad press.

The computerized voice of the navigation system announced the approaching exit number and instructions, and Sophia stayed in the right lane for the exit. As the voice related the next direction and turn, she continued around the curve of the ramp, merging onto the frontage road. She glanced ahead, noting the absolute darkness surrounding her destination. The Reserve Center would be long closed and the protected forest wouldn't be lit, either. Whoever had brought her here would have to speak to her through the car window. She had no intention of getting out and making herself an easier target.

A screech and scream of tires against the

pavement brought her attention back to the road immediately. A car in front of her squealed to an abrupt stop. She checked her mirrors, her options limited by the traffic in the other lane, and jerked the wheel. She swerved right onto the rough shoulder so she wouldn't plow into the car. At nearly fifty miles per hour, her tires growled over the rumble strip cut into the pavement. She missed the stopped car by mere inches and braked hard, desperate to stop safely on the shoulder and catch her breath.

The driver in the stopped car suddenly gunned the engine and swerved to the shoulder, pushing his fender into her car. What the hell?

She couldn't see the driver through the tinted windows, but there was no way he hadn't seen her car. Dumbfounded, she swore again as she urged her car forward to escape. It didn't work. She braked, hoping he'd drive by. No such luck. Metal scraped and she was caught, helpless, as the other car forced hers off the road and down into the tree-lined ditch.

As her car slid down the slope, the other driver left her. Sophia struggled to get her car level and back up to the safety of the roadway. With the car off balance, the rear end fishtailed as her tires lost traction in the longer grass. She tried turning one way, then the other, only to find a loose bit of terrain that sent her car sliding farther into a ditch she hadn't seen. The seat belt grabbed at her, holding her tight until the car finally slid to a stop.

Thankfully the air bag didn't deploy. The navigation system warned she was going the wrong way. With shaking hands she silenced the automated voice grating out route corrections. Her headlights were swallowed by the ditch while the lights of other vehicles cut through the darkness on the highway above.

She twisted in the seat, looking for any sign of the other car. Apparently, it was long gone. Furious, she unfastened her seat belt and leaned over to scoop up her phone and purse from the passenger-side floorboard.

Suddenly the passenger door opened and the bright beam of a flashlight made her wince and shy away. "Hurry, Sophie." A hand stretched out to her from the other side of that glaring light.

The voice… *Impossible. Sophie?* Only Frank had ever gotten away with calling her Sophie.

She froze, too startled to move or reply. Maybe she'd hit her head. Maybe she'd been killed and didn't realize it yet.

"Move it!" The sharp command left no room for debate. "We have to get out of here right now."

The urgency in his voice seemed at odds with what must be a hallucination. If, somewhere deep in her subconscious, she hoped for help from her dead husband, wouldn't he be as calm as he'd been through every stress during their life together?

"Snap out of it." He tugged on her free hand. "Or they'll kill us both."

She couldn't see his face, though his touch felt familiar. "You're already dead," she whispered.

"Not anymore," he said, his tone gentling.

First the notes, now this...

What was going on? A terrible hoax was the only explanation. Who would do such a thing? "Go away." She resisted the warmth in his voice. The sense of awareness was a figment of her imagination. "Go away!" Panic swelled inside, expanding outward until she thought her skin would shred from the pressure. "Leave me alone!"

Engines roared closer and faded away, cars of all sizes going on about their business as if reality hadn't spun her world out of control. She snatched up her purse and reached to open her door.

It was jammed. Of course it was jammed; the other car had damaged the driver's side of her car.

"This way. Now!" The man who couldn't be her husband swore as she continued to fight with the door that wouldn't budge.

"That's enough." The flashlight went out. He grabbed her arm and dragged her across the seats and out of the car.

The crush of his fingers burned her skin with undeniable familiarity. She told herself to fight him, told herself she was delusional, and still her body refused to resist.

When her feet hit the ground, she wobbled a bit, whether a result of the shock, the panic or the uneven ground, she couldn't be sure. Probably all of the above. Her determined rescuer steadied her body with his, and in the shadows she recognized the shape and scent of the man who'd been her partner in life for three decades. Impossible…

"Frank?" In the darkness it was hard to tell. Maybe her vision had been compromised along with her common sense. "How?"

"I'll explain everything in a minute. Can you walk?"

"Of course." Offended, she took a step as he did, then stopped short. "My suitcase!" Her computer was in there; she wouldn't leave it behind. "It's in the back."

"At least you came prepared to run." He sounded relieved as he returned to pull her suitcase out of the backseat. "Tell me you didn't check out of the hotel."

She hadn't, though she refused to volunteer anything. "I don't owe *you* any explanations."

"True enough."

She struggled to keep up with his longer stride even in her flats. *Just like old times*, she thought. At just over six foot he was eight inches taller than her, and those inches seemed to all be in his legs. Where were they going? Away from her car...back the way she'd come, she realized. The headlights of a car in the distance allowed her to make out a vehicle waiting in the ditch a few yards away. Black. SUV.

He opened the passenger-side door for her, the way he'd done at every opportunity since their first date. Her stomach churned as her heart floated on a silly, girlish burst of hope. Could this really be Frank, alive and apparently well? She squashed the fluttery sensations. If it was, her husband owed her a great many answers. "Where are you taking me?"

"Does it matter as long as you survive?"

"It might," she replied. "I can take care of myself, you know."

"One of the many things I love about you."

Though he'd surely meant it as a comfort, his use of the present tense deflated her hopes and sent them crashing in an unwelcome thud in her chest. It couldn't be true. If he still loved her, why had he let her suffer thinking he was dead? "The rental agreement is in the car," she remembered, too late.

The SUV bumped and lurched along the ditch until he found enough of a rut to get them back up to the road. "Sophie, they know you were driving the car. You were run off the road because they were following your movements. They've *targeted* you."

She studied what she could see of his hard profile, finally registering his all-black attire. In the dark sweater, cargo pants and matte jump boots, he'd dressed for an operation rather than a reunion. She suppressed the chill of concern about what he'd gotten himself tangled up in. "Who is 'they'?"

"It's a long story."

"Then start talking." How could this be happening?

"As soon as we're safely out of here. The story I have to tell you is too important to be interrupted."

"Convenient." She crossed her arms. "You invite me to a conversation and then you won't talk."

"It's better if you hear *none* of it rather than only some of it," he insisted. "Keep an eye out for anyone on our tail."

"Fine." She wanted to ignore him and the outrageous situation, but she couldn't afford such a childish indulgence. "At least tell me how you faked your death."

"Soon, I promise."

Anger surged through her, fueled by the adrenaline of sliding off the road into increasingly impossible circumstances. "Tell me now or take me back to the hotel."

"If I take you back to the hotel, they'll kill you tonight," he claimed. "And Frankie tomorrow."

That got her attention and put her focus back on point. She pulled her cell phone out of her purse, her fingers brushing, in the process, the notes he'd written. Goose bumps surged up and down her arms. "I'm calling Victoria. She'll send someone to pick us up."

He shook his head. "No. Turn it off. Please," he added, softening the order to a request. "There's no such thing as safe if they can track you."

She'd deactivated the GPS signal, but he didn't need to know that. Until she could trust him, she wouldn't give him any more advantages. Let him worry that she could turn on her phone at any time and get help immediately. "Give me a good reason to trust anything coming out of your mouth."

"I'm your husband," he stated. "You've always been my top priority."

She laughed. "I might believe such a statement if you were still officially *alive*." Headlights flashed in the side mirror, and her heart rate kicked up. She hoped it was just a speeder and not more trouble.

"Then how about this?" He spared her a quick glance. "I'm the only living person who understands what we're up against."

The "we're" stood out to her, a beacon slicing through the fog of his words. Reluctantly, she cooperated, turning off her phone and dropping it into her purse again.

"You're angry." He checked his mirrors. "You should be. And I'm more sorry than any words can accurately convey."

"That sounds like a cop-out." She ignored the little voice in her head that wanted to give him the benefit of the doubt. Faking a suicide fell into the category of drastic measures. Frank wasn't the sort to take such a step without good cause. She fisted her hands in her lap, her fingernails digging into her palms. If she left her hands loose, she would no doubt reach out to him just to see if he was real.

"At the time, it was necessary," he said as if he knew what she was thinking. "I knew you'd be okay, better off without me dragging you down."

What did that mean? She heard the bitterness underscoring his words. If she was so much better off, why storm back into her life? Why were she and Frankie in danger? "Being a widow hasn't been peaches and cream, Frank." Her emotions leaped wildly with every heartbeat, unable to settle between joy that he was alive and outrage that he'd chosen a fake death rather than trust her with his secrets. How dare he!

"Yeah, well, being dead isn't all it's cracked up to be, either."

"You've put Frankie and me through terrible heartache. She needed you." *I needed you.* She kept the admission to herself, unwilling to let him have that much of her again. Not before she understood how this had happened.

"You both need me right now." He sighed and in the light of oncoming headlights she caught the tic in his jaw.

"Arrogant as ever." She couldn't resist baiting him. That supreme confidence had been simultaneously one of his most attractive and most frustrating traits when they were young and eager to get out and conquer the world. *Together.* So much for that philosophy serving as the cornerstone of their marriage and family.

False or not, death had parted them, and he'd left her alone to find her own way through the consequences of his mistakes. "You know I can keep a secret," she said, hating the tremor in her voice. "You had no right to keep the truth from me."

"I know." He stretched a hand toward her as he used to do on road trips. "I'm so sorry, *dolcezza*."

She didn't take that hand, though refusing it cost her. She wanted to touch him so badly. "You're going to tell me the whole story." He'd never been a fan of her using an inflection that carried the same gravity and certainty of his general's tone of command, but if any situation required it, this was the one.

"I am," he replied, with both hands on the steering wheel once more. "You're not going to like it."

"I already don't like it, Frank."

He'd saved her life tonight. In theory, anyway. For all she knew, he'd hired the driver to run her off the road so he could look like a hero. She gave herself a mental shake. Regardless of circumstances, she couldn't believe he would willfully risk her safety under any circumstances.

"Give me one thing," she said. "One detail

to go on, or I will call Victoria and Frankie and tell them you've kidnapped me."

He muttered an oath, knowing she would follow through. Between the Colby Agency and Leo Solutions, Frank wouldn't have anywhere to hide if they knew he was alive.

"The man following you was one of the top snipers in the Afghanistan military. One word from his boss and your life is over."

She sucked in a breath. "Why?" Who would make her a target?

"That's one detail. I swear to you, as soon as I'm sure we're out of harm's way, I'll tell you everything."

"Harm's way or not, you'll tell me everything tonight." He wasn't the only one who could issue orders.

With a short nod, he rolled his broad shoulders, shifting in the seat as he followed the signs toward Chicago Midway International Airport.

She remembered the feel of those shoulders under her hands after a tough day at work when she'd help him work out the kinks…or late at night in the heat of passion. Oh, how she wanted to trust him, to be sure she could trust him. It scared her—more than being run off the road—just how much she wanted to believe in Frank Leone again.

Chapter Three

When Frank was convinced they hadn't been followed, he decided on a mid-priced hotel near the airport. If they didn't take cash, he had a credit card that matched his false ID. Although Sophia probably wouldn't have complained about the dirt-cheap place where he'd been staying, he didn't want to risk taking her there. If the enemy was this close, anything could happen.

Besides, he couldn't imagine the woman he loved so dearly, with her timeless sense of style, in that flea-bitten decor. The discussion ahead of him would be difficult enough without any guilt over the accommodations. He was distracted plenty by her amazing body. He'd missed her so much. She deserved the best life could offer. Whether she wanted to accept protection from him right now or not, he had to make sure she stayed safe.

Knowing his wife, he suspected their marriage was beyond salvaging. He'd never win back her trust—not in the ways that mattered most. Over three decades ago he'd marveled that the smartest, prettiest girl in the world had fallen in love with him and stuck by him through an army career that carried them around the globe. There had never been any real secrets between them until those last two years. This entire mess rested on his shoulders. *All of it was his fault.*

No avoiding the hard reality of truth. He could offer explanations and apologies—and he would—even knowing it wouldn't make any difference in the long run. He'd started this journey with the best of intentions and it had backfired completely. His mistakes had already cost him the love of his life; he'd never forgive himself if his mistakes got her and their daughter hurt or killed.

Two years ago, she'd sensed the distance he had created to shelter her. Worse, he'd sensed her doubts. That unexpected result had hurt him the most. The wariness he'd seen in her eyes during their last visit, after the guilty verdict had been announced, had plagued him through every lonely day since he'd disappeared.

He parked at the back of the building and

came around to open her door, taking her suitcase as she exited the SUV. Finally, he indulged himself with an up-close study of her. Sophia created a fashion statement in any circumstance. Her black sweater and perfectly tailored slacks graced her curves. The long necklace she wore shimmered against the black and he noticed she'd changed from the heels she'd worn to dinner to sleek flats. His arms ached to gather her into a hug, to hold her close and never let go. Without the heels, the top of her head would tuck perfectly under his chin. Despite the memories of how comforting that embrace would be, he managed to keep his distance.

When they were safe behind the locked door of the rented room, he breathed a little easier. If they were lucky, they would survive the night and he could get her on a plane to the tropics tomorrow. He wanted her far away from the inevitable conflict on the horizon.

He dropped her suitcase on the bed, ignoring that potential minefield, while she strolled on by and pulled a chair away from the table. He heard her fidgeting a bit, settling in while she waited for him to explain himself. He didn't have to look to know she had her right leg crossed over her left, her hands linked in her lap.

Where to begin? He studied his hands, not quite ready to face her. "Do you want a drink?"

"No, thank you."

Her voice was cool, aloof, and he could feel her big brown eyes studying him. He sighed. It shouldn't be this hard to talk to his *wife*. On some level he believed she might understand. Too bad that level was smothered by guilt.

"Just get on with it," she urged in the unflappable tone that had guided professional and family meetings with equal efficiency. "I want the truth. The whole truth." She shook her head, the one visible concession to her anger and frustration. "Some sort of reasonable explanation for what you've done to us."

He closed his eyes a moment, pushing a hand through hair that felt too long since he'd abandoned the shorter army regulation cut. "I doubt much of what I'm about to say will sound reasonable."

The silence stretched between them like a high wire over the Grand Canyon, and he was walking without a net. There'd been no training or experience to prepare him for this crisis. "I did what I believed was necessary to protect you and Frankie." He'd allowed his professional life to destroy his family. No excuses would suffice and none of the words in his mind felt adequate to the task. On a deep breath, he perched on the side of the bed closer to her chair. "It started before we moved to Washington," he began, watching the awareness come into her lovely eyes. "Keeping you out of it was essential."

"Because you planned to become a traitor?"

"Never." He winced. "Though I knew it was possible my actions would look that way."

She caught her full lower lip between her teeth. "Your daughter never believed you were capable of treason," she said. "Unfortunately, by that time, I didn't share her confidence."

He deserved that for how poorly he'd handled the situation. "I wanted to explain, to reassure you." The risks had been too great. Any out-of-character reaction from Sophia would have tipped off the criminals the army had been trying to root out. "You couldn't have helped me. I looked at it from every angle. If I'd told you anything at all, if you'd reacted too much or not enough, if you'd changed your analysis or assessment, it would've gotten all three of us killed."

"What happened?" She hurled the words at him. "Names and dates, Frank." She leaned forward, pinned him with those wary eyes. "Give me a clear and accurate picture. Did you know Frankie believed I willfully helped convict you?"

"No!" He pushed to his feet, striding as far from her as the room allowed. He hadn't understood why his daughter had wound up working in Savannah when Sophia launched the new business in Seattle, but he couldn't risk getting close enough to either of them to find out. "How could she believe such a thing?"

"You can ask her yourself. Now keep talking," she said. "Hold back now and I'll walk right out that door and in my heart you'll stay dead forever."

Sophia didn't make idle threats. If she walked out of this room without the details, without his protection, she'd be dead within the week. Frankie, too. "It's too dangerous. Please, believe that if nothing else."

She drummed her fingertips impatiently on her knee.

He crossed the room again, forcing himself to sit down at the table. He could slow down and do this right. "First, I'm not a traitor." He stopped right there as the emotion choked him. He didn't know quite how to beg her forgiveness, to uproot the terrible seeds of doubts he'd planted. "The Army Criminal Investigations Command approached me just over two years ago." Though he knew all deals were off, his voice cracked on exposing her to the black stain that had ended his career. "Before that last deployment. Equipment had gone missing. Locals claimed army personnel were helping move drug shipments. High-value targets disappeared without a trace. While that sounds logical with the honeycomb of hideouts in Afghanistan, no rumors or sightings were getting out. CID asked me to go undercover and appear amenable to cooperating with one particular drug lord. I did what was required of me, as always."

She gasped, her eyes wide and sad. "The CID didn't back you up?"

"That was *before* the treason charge." He knew she was thinking about the lives lost on that last busted mission. "Cooperating with the drug lord was a test to earn the trust of the criminals CID wanted to net. What I didn't realize at the time was that by passing that test I put you and Frankie in danger." He hitched his shoulders against the impossible burden. "Smoothing the way for that drug shipment earned me a rare invitation to Hellfire, an elite circle of retired military personnel that CID had been trying to dismantle for more than five years."

She stared at him in disbelief. "They named themselves after a missile?"

He nodded. "They're cocky. Considering what they've gotten away with and how they've managed to line their pockets, they've earned the moniker. As a general willing to cross the line for personal gain, I was a shoo-in. Once I was in, my real goal was to identify the Hellfire leadership and gather evidence against them."

"Which meant working with them in the short-term," she said quietly.

"Yes." He swallowed the lump of guilt in his throat. Good men had died for bad reasons that day. Undercover or not, he'd been ready to serve time as a penance. "And it eventually led to the treason charge." He cracked his knuckles. "There was a bank account in the Caymans that would've made you blush." His stilted laughter didn't hold any humor. "Doing bad things for the right reasons is no excuse. I should've found another way."

The CID special agent running his part of the operation assured him there hadn't been another way, but he would carry those terrible memories forever. On his feet again, Frank paced to the door and back, his mind lost in that cursed patch of dirt and the acrid scents of burning fuel and explosives roiling through the desert air.

With both hands fisting helplessly at his sides, he forced himself to tell her the rest. "We figured out after that fiasco, I wasn't the only CID recruit. Another team was tracking the drug shipment. Somehow Hellfire learned the shipment would be seized and used the opportunity to blame it on me."

"Moving illegal drugs is a crime, yes. That doesn't explain the treason charge."

He rubbed one thumb hard into the palm of his other hand. "Hellfire scrubbed the op rather than risk exposure. As Hellfire's newest member, I took the rap for the whole deal, letting the real traitors get away clean, their drug money gushing again like crude oil from a new well less than a week later."

"Frank, if what you say is true, it wasn't your fault."

Of course it was. He looked down to find she'd moved too close, her hands holding his. He wasn't worthy of her sympathy. Reluctantly, he shifted out of her reach. "The treason charge was manufactured just to ruin me, in case I was inclined to flip on Hellfire."

"I didn't want to believe you'd sold information about troop movements and weapons in Kabul, but who else could have leaked those facts?"

Only another general and his cronies, Frank kept to himself. As an analyst, she would've assessed and reported on the intel provided. That was the trouble. With Hellfire railroading him and manipulating the intel, the only possible verdict was guilty.

"I had to do something. Behind bars, I'd never get to the bottom of this, if they even let me live. My CID contact, Special Agent J.D. Torres, came to see me after the verdict and we devised a plan to fake my death. Once I escaped, I knew enough to keep gathering evidence against them without worrying that they'd go after my family."

"And yet here we are, almost a year later." She sank back into the chair.

"Yes." His worst nightmare coming true in full color and in real time. "Based on what I learned during my brief time within Hellfire, I've been piecing parts of the puzzle together. I've learned how the drugs come into the country and I know the top three players in the group. I even managed to stop a drug shipment last month."

"That's progress, I guess. What did Torres have to say?"

He recognized that look. She was shifting gears, playing devil's advocate. He was about to preempt that move. "Torres was the only person who knew about me. I reached out to him to turn in my latest report and let him know where I stashed Hellfire's drugs for the CID to clean up. He didn't respond. I discovered he died in a single-car wreck last month. He'd gone missing more than forty-eight hours before police found the car torched, just off his normal route to and from work. Taking that shipment managed to get another man killed and put you and Frankie in the crosshairs."

"How can they possibly know you were responsible?"

"Process of elimination," he replied. "I'm the only one who understands how the money and drugs move through their sick, private retirement fund. I can't be sure when they learned I'm alive. They must have tortured Torres to discover how we stayed in contact."

"They threatened Frankie and me to draw you out?" She closed her eyes, her fingers sliding the pendant of her necklace along the chain. "How did they tell you?"

"It was a private message on a social media account. They sent me a picture of you, then followed that with the kill order." When she let loose a string of Italian curses for Hellfire, he couldn't have agreed more. "I can't quit now. If I don't stop them, who knows how many more people will get hurt or die while they get richer?"

Her gaze was distant, thoughtful, as she resumed her place at the very edge of her chair. "I felt someone watching me in Chicago."

"Yes," he said with a nod. "I've been shadowing the man they put on you since you arrived this morning. I had to move fast before the sniper could set up the shot."

"So you pulled me out of harm's way."

"It almost worked perfectly." His heart had stopped when they'd forced her off the road. "I'm not sure why they ran you off the road, unless they wanted your death to look like an accident."

"What about Frankie?"

The edge of panic in her voice slid as deep as a blade between his ribs. "I'm hoping this fiancé of hers can watch her back, but the sooner I wrap this up, the better for everyone." Once he eliminated Hellfire and knew his girls were safe, he could think about what to do with the rest of his lonely life.

Sophia nodded, her face pinched as she laced her fingers together in her lap. There had been a time when they'd faced bad news hand in hand. He never should have kept any of this from her. "Is he a good man?"

She lifted her gaze to meet his, blinking as she tried to put his question into the proper context. "Aidan? He's the best. Did you know he was a Colby investigator?"

"Yes. I did a background search on him." While Frank respected Victoria Colby-Camp and her agency, this was his baby girl's life on the line. "I sent him a death threat today."

"You did *what*?"

"Well, I sent it to him, but it was aimed specifically at Frankie," he clarified, realizing too late he'd only made things worse. "I wanted them on alert. I couldn't blurt out what was really going on. I needed them to react quickly, not ask questions."

"Oh, Lord." Her expressive eyes rolled to the ceiling. "Here I was, trying to figure out how to clue her in that you're alive and that we might need her help."

"We can't do that. We can't tell her anything." Panic snapped and clawed at his heart. "The more she knows about me, the more danger she's in."

Sophia's sound of frustration mimicked an unhappy grizzly bear. "If I don't kill you before this is over, she will. Trust me on that."

"I deserve it," he said through another wave of anguish. "But if I don't stop them—"

She held up a hand. "I can fill in the blank." She massaged the lobes of her ears around her earrings. "The treason charge," she began. "Did you knowingly send that team in Kabul to their deaths?"

That she could even think it of him stopped his heart more effectively than the drug he'd used to fake his death. Still, in light of everything, it was a fair question. "I did not." It had been such a sharp edge he'd been walking and he thought he'd done everything possible to make sure only he would or could be injured. A tactic that left him with no allies when the plan backfired. He'd been too new, hadn't known the real players within Hellfire or the full measure of their greed.

Now he did, and he needed to give his wife and daughter the best protection. "I know you don't owe me anything, *dolcezza*. Not your understanding and certainly not your forgiveness."

"Be quiet. I'm thinking of our next step."

"Our?" he echoed, staring at her. "No way."

"You need me," she countered.

He did need her. Desperately. When this was over, maybe they could talk about just how badly he needed her. Assuming he lived through the fight Hellfire would present. "What I need most is to know you're tucked away safely out of Hellfire's reach."

"Is there such a place?"

He didn't say yes fast enough.

"Then we'll do this together," she declared. She stood, the ghost of a smile tipping her lush mouth.

"Absolutely not," he said. He wanted to

keep her as far from the chaos as possible. He'd often fantasized about a reunion when the coast was clear. Coming home to Sophia had always been the best part of fulfilling his military responsibilities. Someday this mess with Hellfire would be behind them and, if she gave him a chance, he'd never leave her again.

"Look where you've wound up working alone!" She switched to Italian, indulging in a fiery rant that called into question his intelligence and sanity. "I have contacts and resources. You need my help."

"You think the two of us can do what the CID couldn't?"

"Yes." Her eyes glittered, daring him to contradict her. "As a team," she said pointedly. "We *were* unstoppable. They have regulations and systems. We have a dead man with good intel and a reputable woman with excellent connections."

He knew that look. In full protective mode, she wouldn't back down, even if it was for her own good. He reconsidered his strategy. "Since we're in Chicago," he said, "why don't we ask if you can work your connections from Victoria's offices?" The Colby Agency could keep Sophia safe while he went after Hellfire personally.

"Just me?" she asked too sweetly.

Naturally she saw straight through him. "Standard protocol," he said, defending the suggestion. "You in the office, me in the field."

She tossed her head. "I will *not* let you out of my sight. Our daughter would never forgive me if something happened to you...*again*."

"She already thinks I'm dead. I refuse to take the chance of making her an orphan for real. I don't want her to know anything until this is done."

She pinned him with a wicked glare. "Were you this melodramatic during official briefings?"

"The lives of my wife and daughter weren't on the line in my official briefings," he said, thoroughly exasperated with her insurmountable stubborn streak. "Haven't you been listening to me?" He'd spent more than twenty years commanding troops, so how was it he had so much trouble with this one woman?

"I have been listening very closely. The only real point you've made is that you need my help."

He scrubbed at the back of his neck. How could he have believed she would listen to reason? He needed help, yes, and he'd count her an excellent ally—from the safety of an office surrounded by armed experts. Putting her in the line of fire was taking an unforgivable chance. Not to mention how keeping her close would be torture. Already her familiar lily-and-sandalwood fragrance seeped into his system, giving him more comfort than he deserved. "You can help me—from a safe distance."

"Frank, be reasonable. You need someone at your back."

"Victoria would agree with me," he countered. As arguments went, it was too weak and they both knew it.

Her gaze sharpened. Her keen mind was working through his protests to the crux of the problem. "You're holding back a significant factor here. Who is it, Frank? Who's at the top of Hellfire?"

Furious at himself more than anyone at how he'd been fooled and used, he studied the pattern in the carpeting. He met her gaze, at last. "Kelly Halloran is the top man."

The blood drained from her face, turning her vibrant golden skin to ash. "Sit down," he said, moving to catch her. She slumped to the edge of the couch, her shoulders hunching as if she could physically block the news. He understood her reaction.

"Why?" she whispered. She sucked in a breath, eased away from him and tried again.

"We've known him forever. We know his children. His wife and I were once close friends." She rubbed her hand over her heart. "They were at our wedding. They brought me flowers when Frankie was born. Our kids played together. He held me when I learned you were... dead."

All the more reason Frank wanted to see that bastard go down. The few inches of space her retreat created left an icy chill on his skin. "This isn't a quick, fly-by-night operation. It's been developing for a long time. So far I haven't figured out what pushed Halloran over the edge."

She bit her lip. "You believe he'd willfully hurt our daughter?"

Frank nodded. "The man he is today? Yes. He'd give that order." He waited for it to dawn on Sophia that their old friend had issued her death order earlier today.

"Oh." She pressed a hand to her stomach. "I could be sick."

He'd felt the same way. "Please don't ask me to make it easier on him by letting you come with me. This is guaranteed to turn ugly, fast."

"It's already ugly," she said, her voice tight. "Kelly Halloran ordered my execution to scare you into silence," she mused. "The bastard."

When she met his gaze, her eyes were clear, her determination shining. "You can't expect me to sit back and watch him run you in circles."

"If that's your idea of encouragement, I don't need any more," he said.

She spread her palms across her knees. "Talk me through everything you have so far and then I'll decide if I can best help from a safe distance or right beside you."

"Now you're in charge?" He wanted to leap on the idea of having an ally, of having her beside him again. If only they weren't going up against a man who knew them both all too well.

"One of us should be." Standing, she crossed the room to her suitcase, pulling out her laptop. "Come on. Catch me up." She rolled her hand, urging him to fill her in while she plugged in the computer.

He marveled at her resilience. He always had. They'd said "for better or worse" on their wedding day and lived it every day since. Until he'd shut her out. She made a good point. So far, going solo had only netted him one easily replaced shipment of drugs. Hardly enough to snare Halloran or put an end to a system as established as Hellfire.

"All right," he said at last. "But I won't be convinced that you should be doing any fieldwork."

Her mouth curved in a smirk. "You will be."

Somehow he was afraid she could be right.

Chapter Four

Breathing in slow and deep, Sophia didn't sit down again until she was sure her stomach wouldn't embarrass her. "Kelly Halloran," she said. Her anger with Frank shifted abruptly to a new target. It was hard to picture one of their oldest and dearest friends orchestrating such an elaborate criminal network, complete with a sniper aiming at her head. "When we find him, I want the first shot."

"I won't let you kill him," Frank countered. "His sorry life isn't worth spending a single day of yours in prison."

She turned at the wariness in his voice. "I didn't mean with a gun. I don't want to kill him. I want to scratch his eyes out, maybe break a rib or two or blow out his knee." Her body hummed with the need to do violence. "He threatened to kill our daughter." The idea of it shocked her almost as much as Frank standing here alive and well. "When I'm done with him, I want him to rot in a dark, slimy little hole for the rest of his days."

Frank gave a low whistle. "Guess I'm lucky you haven't torn me apart."

"The night is still young." She sent him a glance full of warning. "If I were you, I wouldn't bring up your grand scheme to tuck me safely away again."

"Duly noted."

"Good. Keep talking and let's see what we can come up with."

She logged on to the internet via the hotel connection and created a new online persona for tonight's research. Assuming Halloran had technical experts with credentials equivalent to those of his renowned assassin, she didn't want to tip them off too soon. Behind her she heard Frank resume his pacing.

Hearing those footfalls made her smile. Pacing hadn't been his habit until after Frankie was born. He'd spent many nights walking up and down the hallways to help her sleep when she was a baby. All these years later, his body went through the soothing motions automatically. She doubted he even noticed.

"We can't go directly at Halloran," he said. "I've tried. That's why I went after the drugs."

She sat back on her heels, nearly afraid to ask. "What do you know about him?"

"His current address is a place outside Phoenix, one of those golf communities tucked behind an elaborate gate and rent-a-cop security."

She brought up an overview image of the area, waiting for him to continue.

"He's insulated," Frank said. "I've been thinking if we could pin down one of the others, someone close to the top, we could force them to roll over on Halloran."

She thought through that approach and dismissed it. "We can see about that if we can find a chink in Hellfire's armor." She pursed her lips. "You said the money goes through a bank in the Caymans. Have you tried following that trail? If we put that kind of information into the right hands, it could make a difference."

"Unless Halloran believes any information leaks come from his own men, he'll know it's me and he'll move to kill Frankie. Is there any way you can urge her to take a vacation?"

Sophia shook her head. "Not without a good explanation. With Paul in prison and me out of the office, she and Aidan need to be present and visible at Leo Solutions."

Frank grumbled his displeasure. Hiding and waiting only gave their enemy more power.

"Tell me about your Cayman account."

"The money isn't there," he said. "They redistributed the cash after I was ousted."

"Do you remember any details?"

He gave her the bank, account number and online log-in information. Within a few minutes, she had the full account history, though the current balance was zero. "They made regular deposits," she observed, noting the dates in a new document for further research later. "I know it's been a long time, but do these deposit dates correspond to any actions that you're aware of?"

He pulled up a chair and they talked through what he remembered about that time, matching what he'd seen overseas with what she was seeing in the bank history. She wasn't sure it would be enough, even if she could get it into the right hands.

"Well, they certainly wouldn't have made deposits only to your account on those days. Gotta love the precision and habits of military men." She made a few more notes as she went along. There were other people—friends in the intelligence and media communities—she could approach if necessary. "Based on these numbers, I can see why Halloran's crew has been so loyal. Getting one of them to roll on him will be a long shot."

"I'm trying to find the right pressure point,"

Frank said. He laced his fingers behind his head and stretched his neck. Another rush of need to touch and soothe him startled her. It had always been so easy to reach out and offer him comfort and support.

It didn't feel right to hold all that in. It didn't feel right to approach him, either. She tamped down the uncertainty. This wasn't her first uncomfortable classified meeting. Her feelings could wait until they'd accomplished the current "mission."

And then what? She had no idea.

"Do you know if he's threatened the families of the others in the group?" She couldn't quite reconcile the friendly Kelly Halloran she remembered with this uncaring criminal. She hadn't missed Frank's refusal to give her the other names of those involved. "Money can't be the only hold he has over them."

"Money can be a big incentive. Any secrets or crimes they committed are long buried."

"Mmm-hmm." She kicked off her shoes, getting comfortable. She was tempted to launch an immediate search into Halloran and stopped herself just in time. The resources at Leo Solutions would make this easier, but she wasn't ready to log in and risk leaving such an obvious trail for Halloran. By now he knew his attack on her had missed and he'd be waiting for some reaction.

"From what you've said, we can't beat them by just interfering with their pipeline. Manipulating the money could work. If we can find a way to tie up their cash—"

"I'm not letting you do anything remotely criminal," he said, scowling at her.

"But it's okay for you to steal drugs and who knows what else?"

He shrugged a shoulder, his blue gaze sliding back to the laptop monitor. "I'm officially dead," he pointed out. "My real name and reputation can't get any worse."

She wanted to shake him. He couldn't have just given up on everything, could he? The best possible outcome here was to restore his name and reputation so he could reclaim his life as a husband and father, as a friend and partner. Already, she could see Frankie's delighted face when she learned her father was alive, healthy and not a convicted traitor.

But could he be her husband again? Sophia's throat attempted to close. Could she be his wife? So much hurt stood between them.

"We could notify the authorities about the next incoming shipment," she said.

Frank's scowl deepened and he covered his eyes. "Based on the schedule, there should be a shipment coming into Seattle in a few days. Which is another reason I think he's targeted you and Frankie. He can't take the chance I'd ask you for help." He leaned forward and tapped his fingers together. "He knows I'm alive and that I know his system."

"And he knows you have his drugs."

"He's behaving as if that's irrelevant," Frank said, clearly troubled by the fact. "He removes the only person who can vouch for me. Then he sits on you and Frankie, issues a kill order, knowing I'll show up."

"Which you did." Thank heaven. She forced her thoughts away from what might have happened if Frank hadn't been so diligent. It took more effort to keep from reaching for her phone to call and check on her daughter.

"His hired gun didn't work very hard to kill either of us." Frank stood up and resumed his pacing. "It's the strangest game of cat and mouse I've ever played and the stakes are too high."

She agreed completely. "You said you've identified the top players. Let's start at the bottom and work our way up."

"Divide and conquer?" He faced her, his dark eyebrows knitting over those clever blue eyes.

"It's a valid strategy for a reason." She smiled,

aiming it at the screen rather than her husband. "There has to be a weak link within Hellfire. Start talking," she said, ignoring the clock in the corner of her monitor. They couldn't stay here indefinitely and, based on the signs of tension radiating from Frank, he was at the end of his rope. Though he might not be ready to admit it, he needed her—or someone—to help him put an end to this nightmare.

Frank turned the chair around and straddled it, bracing his arms along the top rail. "I backed up my handwritten notes to a cloud server."

She brought up the website and he gave her the username and password as if they were random, but her fingers stuttered in recognition. He'd used the day and date of her first miscarriage for those fields. No one even knew about that except the two of them. She hadn't been far enough along to share the news yet.

She told herself to say something and couldn't find sufficient words. If a single shred of doubt had existed inside her that this man was her husband, it was gone now.

"I've been tracking movements and making connections for months," he said as if she hadn't noticed. "If this was my pet project, Darren Lowry would worry me most. He was on Halloran's staff for a few years."

"Go on," she encouraged as she opened another tab and typed the name into her search engine. As Frank gave her the details he knew about Lowry's background, Sophia's determination firmed.

This would be so much easier with the assets at the office, but she couldn't think about that yet. Much as Halloran had pulled Frank out of hiding, she wanted to draw any confrontation away from Seattle and their daughter.

"Is this the same Lowry, retired four years ago? This report has a Darren Lowry under investigation for sexual misconduct in Iraq on his second tour." She leaned to the side to give Frank a better look at the pictures she'd brought up on the screen.

"Same guy," Frank confirmed. "Maybe the charges were fabricated against him, too."

Sophia's lip curled and her mouth went dry as she read through the report. She kept digging, using Frank's information and online sources. She found a current address and the press release when Lowry had been hired by a defense contractor based in Washington, DC, after retiring from the army.

"Could I have some water please?" She didn't want Frank nearby when she logged in to an administrative email account for a law firm website in DC. Leo Solutions had handled the security for one of her oldest friends when he transitioned to private practice after fulfilling his military commitment in the army's Judge Advocate General's Corps. She wasn't doing anything particularly illegal, though Frank wouldn't be happy. Assuming her friend was in town and Frank cooperated, she could follow up tonight's discreet inquiry in person tomorrow.

She accepted the glass of water from Frank and chose her next words carefully. "I have a friend in DC who can give us some guidance about how to exploit that old complaint against Lowry," she said, tracing the rim of the water glass. "I'm thinking we cast an ugly spotlight on the skeletons in his closet and make the old fogies of Hellfire sweat a little. It's a fair response to what happened near Parkhurst today."

He sat down across from her, his intense gaze holding hers. "You want Halloran to know we can get to his people, too."

"Exactly."

She struggled to keep her mind on point while her eyes devoured the face that had meant so much to her for more than half of her life. She remembered how those laugh lines had added character to his face, year after year. Anger, raw and cold, surged through her veins.

If Halloran hadn't upped the stakes, would Frank have kept tabs on her at all? Would he have watched her grow old from a distance, without ever allowing her to know he was out there?

Something that resembled dismay flickered across his face. "You're angry."

Of course he could read her changing expressions. He'd always been too good at that. "It comes in waves," she admitted. She dismissed it with a flick of her fingers. Throwing a tantrum wouldn't help either of them. If they successfully dismantled Hellfire, she could be mad at Frank personally for the rest of her life. "Lowry first," she said through gritted teeth.

He bobbed his chin slowly as if uncertain about agreeing with her. "What do you hope to get out of your contact in DC?"

"I won't know for sure until I get there," she hedged while she opened more searches, this time exploring the contractor who had hired Lowry.

"You mean you don't intend to tell me."

"Can you blame me?" She tucked her hands under her legs, squashing the urge to throw something at him. "After what you've described, we need more intel to involve the authorities and take down Halloran the right way. I want him to rot in prison, not slip through the system to lounge about on a sunny island beach."

"I want him to rot, too," Frank said.

She knew that tone. "Not six feet under," she said briskly. "If I can't kill him, neither can you. The bastard isn't worth either of us spending any time in jail." However things worked out between them personally, she wanted to be clear on that point.

She fumed when he sat there silently studying his hands. "That was your plan?"

He opened his mouth, but she cut off his reply. "It would be fine if you killed him because you were already dead and out of our lives?" she demanded. Furious, she clamped her lips together before she said something too terrible to retract. "I must question your logic," she managed.

"If Halloran is dead, he can't give an order to hurt you or Frankie."

"Funny. You were dead and that hurt us plenty."

He reeled back as if she'd slapped him. She would not regret it. The harsh words needed to be said. "We're going to DC, Frank."

"It's a huge risk."

"Do you know how determined Frankie was to clear your name? Do you have any idea?" She didn't wait for a reply. "You saved me tonight and I'm grateful, but I won't sit back and let you disappear again. I won't take on Hellfire in half measures that leave you hanging in some legal limbo. We're going to DC so I can discuss this with a friend I trust."

FRANK TRIED TO ignore the sting of her trusting someone else more than she trusted him, even though her instincts were spot-on. He didn't ask her for the name of her friend. She wouldn't tell him anyway. Shouldn't, in fact. Sophia's connections ran deep thanks to her analysis work with the CIA and others in the alphabet soup of DC. It pissed him off the way Halloran had managed to twist Sophia's analyses against him during the treason trial.

"I believe my friend can help us," she said, her anger having ebbed once more.

He admired her ability to ride through the emotions. He wasn't having nearly the same success. If he got too close, he wanted to take her in his arms and be closer. If he shared a little, he wanted to tell her everything. "In what way?"

She pressed her fingers to her temples and dropped her gaze. "At this point it's only an educated guess. Can't you extend me a little faith and leeway for a day or two?"

"Of course."

Her confidence didn't surprise him. It had been one of her most attractive traits. At the moment her confidence gave his a boost. He refused to be the thundercloud rumbling with doom and gloom in the distance, threatening to rain on every hopeful step forward. He didn't have to tell her he'd make a plan for the worst-case scenario while she was seeking help. She knew him well enough to expect him to come up with a contingency.

"I'll book the flight," he said, pulling out his cell phone and calling the airline he'd used most frequently with his bogus identification. "Wait." He disconnected the call before a reservations agent picked up. "You can't go as you."

"I don't have much choice," she said. "We don't have the time for an alternate identification to be made."

"Victoria knows people. She could help, couldn't she?"

Sophia sighed. "You know the best work takes time. Do you really want to sit here and wait for Halloran to make the next move?"

"No." None of their limited options appealed to him. "We'll drive out. We can leave early—"

"And waste half a day? How does that work in our favor? If Frankie is in danger, we need to move quickly to trap Halloran."

His stomach tightened again. Halloran would stop at nothing to protect his retirement cash cow. Another man's family wasn't nearly as valuable as an endless flow of money and power.

It had been tough enough for Frank to live without his girls when he thought he was keeping them safe. If the distance were permanent, if by some twist of fate he had to go on breathing, knowing his mistakes meant their lives had been cut short…

"Frank?" Sophia's voice brought him back from that bleak abyss he'd been staring into. "Talk to me."

He rolled his shoulders. "They ran you off the road. I'm sure they know I rescued you." He wouldn't sleep at all tonight, waiting for one of Halloran's thugs to track the rental car and break down the door.

"Look around, Frank. You created a safe place. They haven't found us yet."

Yet. The word echoed through his head. Every way he looked at it, Halloran had the advantage.

"We have to take the chance," she said. "You're obviously worried. What can they really do between now and morning?"

Considering Halloran's established organization, Frank could think of several bad examples, none of which he wanted to outline for her in any great detail.

"Our best choice is not to circle the wagons. He'd expect that of me," she said. "He knows how devoted I am—we are—to Frankie. He has to be confused. I didn't run back to my hotel, contact Victoria or call Frankie. All things I should've done if I encountered trouble in Chicago."

"All of which points like a neon arrow to my involvement in your rescue."

"Yes. They probably watched you pull me out of there somehow. More important, where would two capable parents run if their daughter was in danger?"

"To her."

She nodded. "Instead, picture his reaction when he learns I went to DC. He'll flip out with the possibilities."

It was a solid approach. So far all he'd been able to do was observe and keep some drugs off the streets. Nothing he'd done seemed to get under Halloran's skin. The man was too confident in his system. "And if we rattle him, you're hoping he makes a mistake."

"The sooner the better for us."

She was right. They had to keep Halloran on edge. Words of gratitude backed up in his throat. Knowing she wasn't doing it for him but for Frankie didn't matter. His wife was back in his life and, for the moment, they were a team.

"All right." He picked up his phone. "Let's book the first flight out."

When they both had confirmation emails about the flight, they discussed tomorrow's plan. He couldn't go with her wherever she was headed. There were too many people who might recognize him. He agreed to stay back and make sure she wasn't followed.

Using tourist maps she pulled up on her screen, they chose rendezvous points and times, and then she closed the computer and tucked it back into her suitcase. Retrieving her cosmetic case and whatever she used for pajamas now, she headed for the bathroom.

While she was busy, he stripped off his sweater and removed his boots and socks. A few minutes later, he heard the bathroom door open and the flick of the light switch. He kept his focus on perfecting the arrangement of an extra pillow and blanket on the small couch, afraid to look her way. The last thing he needed was a refresher course on how alluring she was at bedtime.

Whenever he was deployed or traveling, those first nights apart from her had always been the worst. He missed the scent of lilies clinging to her skin after she applied her favorite lotion. Longed for the feel of her bare feet caressing his calf as she snuggled into his embrace. He couldn't say he'd taken her for granted; the frequent times apart prevented that. No, he'd simply assumed coming home to her was always an option.

"I'd planned to take the couch," she said, rooted in place between the bathroom and the bed.

He turned, pulled by a force he couldn't fight. From the moment he'd dragged her out of the car, he felt a craving to soak her in, as though he could somehow carry a bit of her with him through the foreseeable loneliness ahead. His mouth watered at the sight of her in one of his old T-shirts, her preferred sleepwear. It wasn't a ploy or some balm to his ego. She'd traveled to Chicago solely to see a friend and she'd packed *that* shirt. Did that have any significance? Should he assume she missed him, too, or was it just a comfort factor? He couldn't stop his eyes from roaming over her from head to toe—her hair down and the hem of the shirt skimming high on her toned thighs. She kept trying to push it lower.

"Take the bed." He gave her a smile, though he thought his jaw would crack from the effort. "I'll be fine over here."

"That's silly. You need more room."

His skin tingled from his scalp to the soles of his feet as she gazed at him. What was he supposed to make of that look? "Don't worry about it. You know I've slept well in far worse."

She came to the corner of the bed and stopped, a worried frown pulling at her eyebrows. "You won't be able to stretch out at all."

"Just take the bed," he said through gritted teeth. Unless she was offering to share. Was that it? It would take a better man than him to turn her down if she was.

She slid between the sheets, putting as much of the bed between them as possible. A clear enough message to keep his distance.

He turned out the last light before he stripped off his undershirt and pants. The gear in the pockets rattled as he set the items within easy reach if trouble found them.

"You know, I should thank Halloran." Her voice drifted across the dark room.

It seemed like a damned poor thing to be thankful for. He stared at the ceiling, creased with a blade of light from the parking lot bleeding through the top of the curtains. "I don't want to ask."

"Without him I might never have seen you again."

Could it be possible that she had missed him

as much as he'd missed her? She'd turned their retirement dream into a profitable reality so quickly. And that damned snake Paul Sterling had moved in on her with equal speed. "Without him, we wouldn't be in this mess to begin with," Frank pointed out.

"True."

He was sure she'd drifted off, leaving him with his thoughts and regrets, when she spoke up again. "After…all that happened," she said, "would you ever have come home to me if my life hadn't been in danger?"

He could hardly stand being in this room, so close and still so far removed from her. "I've been searching for a way home to you ever since." He stifled a groan as the truth slipped out. A lie that would guarantee some detachment would've been the smarter move. He'd hurt her so badly it was a miracle she hadn't had him drawn and quartered yet.

He heard the mattress shift and he imagined she'd rolled to her side. He remembered the way she curled her hands around her pillow, her face relaxed and her knees pulled up a little, one foot free of the bedding, serving as a thermostat. Countless mornings in their marriage he'd pressed a kiss to her cheek and left her in just that pose. Every morning since going undercover, he'd regretted his decision to push her away in favor of the job. Now he'd dragged her into an unsanctioned investigation that could wind up destroying both of them.

On the books it appeared as though he'd put his duty to country ahead of his family. Not unexpected for a career officer even though it wasn't spelled out in those exact words in the official oath of service. He'd made an unbearable choice with his family in mind, though they would heartily disagree. No matter the cost, men like Halloran couldn't be allowed to run roughshod over the world. Soldiers and civilians had died for the wrong reasons, thanks to Halloran and his Hellfire group, and Frank meant to right that wrong.

Early on, Frank had been so damned confident no price was too high to bring Halloran to justice. Long before the empty casket had been lowered into the ground, he'd realized his error.

Solitude had been his greatest enemy. He hadn't taken Sophia for granted in their marriage, not as a person or partner. No, but he'd drastically underestimated the strength he gained merely knowing she was on his side, available to talk or listen as needed.

Her breathing evened out and he didn't have the heart to wake her. It was too late to thank her for standing by him during the trial anyway.

The only thing he knew to do was keep pushing forward, as a team, despite the undercurrents of hurt between them. If he could bear the distraction, which was the risk of working with her, they might just reduce Hellfire to ashes.

Chapter Five

The flight was nearly into its descent before Frank relaxed. All night he'd slept with one eye open, expecting an attack on the hotel. At the airport, he kept looking over his shoulder, even past the security checkpoint, certain one of Halloran's goons would make a grab for Sophia. Unless he was completely off his game, they were heading to DC without any Hellfire eyes on them. He wasn't sure what to think, so he tried to be grateful for the momentary reprieve.

Still, with no trouble in Chicago, spies were likely waiting for them in DC. It couldn't be helped—Sophia had to travel as herself right now. They could only move as quickly as possible and leave a trail for Halloran to get worried about. With his ball cap pulled low over his face, Frank had pretended to sleep while keeping an eye on her dark hair several rows ahead of him.

Their arrival in Dulles and the rental car pickup all went without a hitch. This much going smoothly made him wary. Hellfire was dialed in tight on Frank now that they knew he was alive, and things would only accelerate when they realized Sophia was helping him.

Following the plan he and Sophia had devised last night, he parked the car in a public garage and she took the metro to her meeting. He fell back once he was sure no one was tailing her. It bothered him to let her go alone, even knowing she could take care of herself on the busier subways. Returning to keep an eye on their primary rendezvous point, he was happy things were clear so far.

Sophia had not volunteered details about meeting her contact, only that she'd send regular text messages and catch up with Frank in front of the Smithsonian Castle at two o'clock. They'd argued the point, last night and again on the way to the airport, until he was forced to concede. As she'd told him repeatedly, he was officially dead and she'd be walking into places where he might be recognized. If the authorities caught Frank too soon, Halloran would have a better chance of skipping the country unscathed.

Still, letting her out of his sight went against everything inside him. His instincts clamored to shelter and protect his wife and daughter, though he knew being obvious about it would push her too hard at this point. A few hours in her company after so much time apart made this necessary absence unbearably worse. He had no idea what he'd do when this was over and Halloran was in custody, no longer a threat to Frank or his family.

Frank wanted his life back; he wanted his wife and daughter.

With a few hours to kill, he ambled between museums and played the part of tourist as memories of Leone family vacations rolled through his mind. He was strolling along, desperate to sink his teeth into some action, when he noticed the man tailing him.

A chill slid down his spine at the thought of Halloran pegging his last clean fake ID, until he remembered how easily Hellfire could track Sophia. Maybe she was right that he'd been at this alone for too long. Frank's pulse leaped at the potential to get some information from the enemy. The challenge was staying calm, letting the man believe Frank hadn't noticed him.

As a career army officer, he hadn't had much training in espionage or spy tactics. Working his way up to general, he'd learned how to assess, observe and stand out. He'd learned to manage his immediate support staff as well as the many units under his command. Blending in, disappearing and operating alone had required practice after his initial escape from prison as a corpse.

The man dogging his heels didn't look familiar. White male, average height and build, medium brown hair, nondescript jacket and jeans. At the current distance, it was impossible to pin down an age range to anything more specific than "over twenty-five."

Frank led the younger man trailing him away from the rendezvous point just in case Sophia returned early. He walked near groups of tourists and then separately, giving him room to make a move. Picking up his pace, he aimed for the metro station and hurried down the stairs, stepping aside to wait for the tail to catch up.

As the younger man hurried by Frank's position, the profile didn't reveal anything helpful about his identity or his affiliation. It had to be one of Halloran's spies. No one else had reason to be this persistent. Frank fell in behind him, keeping out of sight.

A train arrived and people jockeyed for position. Frank stepped up behind the younger man and shoved the knuckles of his fist into his back. "Looking for me?"

Caught, his shoulders slumped. "You're getting better at this, Leone."

"As if I care about your opinion." Up close, he realized the spy was even younger than he'd guessed at first. Probably a recent washout from one of the elite military teams, searching for a way to clear the chip off his shoulder.

Frank struggled against his first instinct to listen and advise. Although he and Sophia had only one child, he'd counseled many young people through the years, urging them to explore one path or another to suit their skills. This wasn't that kind of meeting.

"You should." The kid tried to look over his shoulder.

"To the right," he said, urging the kid closer to the nearest trash can. "Unload any weapons."

"If they'd sent me to kill you," the kid said, dropping a knife and a handgun into the trash can, "you'd be dead already."

Frank ignored him, pulling a cell phone out of the kid's rear pocket while he was distracted. The warning sounded for final boarding and he gave the kid another shove. "Get on the train."

"I knew you weren't armed," the kid challenged.

"If you know me at all," Frank retorted, "you know I don't need to be."

With a terse nod, the kid obediently surged forward, joining the last stragglers to board the train.

"Who sent you?" Frank asked when they were seated and the train was under way. Part of him hoped it was a federal agency rather than a criminal operation.

"You already know the answer." The kid shook his head. "If you'd recommit, I wouldn't be your enemy. You'd have support, a way out. Face it, you need it."

Frank glared at him.

"No one wants to hurt your family. Cooperate and the danger goes away."

"Cooperate how?" Frank asked, willing to play along for a few minutes. He could just imagine what hellish task Halloran had dreamed up for him to prove his renewed loyalty to Hellfire. "The last time I cooperated, your boss hung me out to dry."

"Ease up," the kid said. "No one was going to leave you in prison. You should've been patient. A man's word is his bond."

Neither Halloran's "word" nor Hellfire's promises had been worth the air wasted to explain them. "Right." Frank calculated the upcoming stops and how long he could keep this kid talking until he had to get back to Sophia. "My wife and daughter were no threat. Your boss started this when he targeted them. You can tell him I'll finish it."

"Hey, you're pissed. I get it." The kid flared his hands wide, then stuck them in his pockets. "Easy to lose the faith considering that nasty treason charge." He kept his voice pitched low. "You keep our secrets and this will still work out according to the original agreement."

The agreement had a small fortune flowing into an offshore bank account in Frank's name and a solitary slice of a private beach in the Caribbean. The same bogus agreement that had left his family believing he committed suicide rather than face justice as a traitor. "I can't ever be me again," he muttered only loud enough for the kid to hear. "No matter what I choose."

"Just so we're clear. Are you threatening Hellfire?"

"No more than they're threatening me," Frank replied.

"That's not the kind of response that makes

the top brass happy. Check your account," the kid said. "A good-faith payment is already there."

"Top brass" implied the kid was working directly for one of the top three retired generals who'd started Hellfire. Maybe Frank could use this—whatever it was—rendezvous to his advantage. He wanted new intel, some solid detail he and Sophia could exploit quickly. He pulled out his cell phone and checked the account. Sure enough, he was wealthy again. Disgust burned in his gut. Halloran had stolen everything from him. Frank's sole purpose now was to take him down, wrapping it up quickly so Frankie and Sophia could live in peace.

The train intercom announced the next stop and people shifted around them, preparing to exit. Frank used the shuffling to lift the kid's wallet. If he could get something helpful out of this kid—something other than an illegal windfall he didn't want—maybe this little detour would prove worthwhile.

Why wasn't the kid asking about Sophia or the missing drug shipment? The question had a new flood of apprehension rushing through Frank.

"I don't know what they have on you," he said quietly, testing the reaction, "but I can help if you come to your senses before the next stop."

The kid snorted. "You can't do a damn thing for me if you're against them." His lip curled like that of a mean dog sizing up his next attack. "I don't want anything from an outsider anyway."

"Is that so?"

"Look, old man, you've got one more chance to be smart."

The "old man" crack was the last straw. Despite being past his prime, Frank had at least one more good fight left in him. He pretended to consider it while he searched for the most expedient route to the finish line. "Call the shooters off my family," Frank demanded, holding out the kid's cell phone.

The kid shook his head, kept his hands in his pockets. "I don't have that authority."

"Then you're no good to me." Frank tucked the phone away. With a quick move, he slid his hand up the kid's arm and pressed on a nerve that turned his arm limp.

"What the hell? Wait, you can't—"

"Just did, son." Frank stood as the train slowed for the next stop. "I've got your wallet, too. If you're smart, you'll hurry to the nearest FBI office and trade information for witness protection before Hellfire learns you've turned on them."

"No." The blood drained from his face, his eyes wide and wild. "You can't do that. Engle would never believe I'd turn."

Frank shrugged. "Belief and trust are fragile things. Good luck." He moved through the doors as the warning sounded, glancing back to see the kid fumbling to get his other arm working.

Engle, Frank thought, mentally tucking the new name away, along with every other word the kid had said. Between the two of them, he was sure he and Sophia would find the connections. He started searching through the kid's phone, knowing it could be a morass of fake IDs and cover stories. Time would tell. If they were lucky, Engle would prove to be a loose link in Hellfire's chain of command.

He glanced at the clock on the display and winced. He had a lot of ground to cover to make the rendezvous point in time. If she thought he'd ditched her—again—there would be hell to pay.

Tuesday, April 19, 2:10 p.m.

SOPHIA WANDERED ON past the Smithsonian Castle when she didn't see Frank in the vicinity.

Frank should be waiting right here, per the plan. She told herself he hadn't left her, that he *would* be here. Wouldn't he?

Or would her husband, in some ill-conceived notion of protecting her, run away again?

She tried to divert the immediate reaction and the negative spiral of her thoughts with what she'd learned in the chat with her old friend Eddie Chandler. It didn't work. Very little from that meeting gave her hope they could successfully expose Halloran's greedy scheme. It would take some creativity and more than a little good luck.

She couldn't give up. Unless they stopped Hellfire, her husband would be forced to live in hiding indefinitely, an outcome she refused to accept. She checked her watch, circled through a nearby garden and turned back. Where was he?

If he had left her, she'd track him down and wring his neck. Though she could hardly be considered abandoned in Washington, DC, even without her resources and connections, that wasn't the point. They'd agreed to move forward together. If he reneged on his word…

No. A cold fear curled into a fist in her belly. He hadn't reneged. She couldn't believe it. If he'd wanted to leave her out of this mess, he would've found a way to leave her in Chicago.

Although it was as clear as the sky above that he hated involving her in this crisis, they'd tossed out any other option. He needed someone helping him unravel Hellfire. He needed her.

She checked the time again, considering the more likely scenarios, each of them increasingly unpleasant as they flashed through her mind. He'd been tailed and led the tail away from her. He'd been recognized and arrested by federal authorities. He'd been killed by Halloran's prize sniper. Her stomach pitched at the ghastly image, putting an end to her terrible thoughts.

If a sniper had struck Frank out here in the Mall, the police and emergency crews would be crawling all over the place by now. Even his arrest would've drawn a media presence.

So, if not killed by a sniper or picked up by police, Frank should be here. The obvious conclusion was he'd spotted someone tailing him. She should move to the alternative rendezvous point, closer to the parking garage. He was probably there, worrying and waiting for her to show up.

He wouldn't leave her. After last night, she was sure he realized he couldn't defeat Hellfire alone. Frank needed her. As much as she needed him, a small voice in her head pointed out with a vicious snarl. It startled her to have that voice reach out and lash at her. She thought she'd left that near-panic intensity locked away in the early days of their marriage.

When they were young, his career path as a military leader had seemed courageous and bold, almost glamorous. His confidence and conviction of purpose had inspired her. Then the reality of life as an officer's wife had surprised her. He'd gone off on one task or another and the urge to cling had been a sharp contrast to her independent nature. Over time, they'd become a stand-out team in his professional life, as well as their family life.

It was the soothing of other wives suffering with similar anxiety that often left her breathless and weepy. For years she had managed the problem alone, only sharing her secret with a therapist. To support her husband, she had to present a strong example. The same fortitude had held true and served her well in her career as an analyst.

She resented being tossed back to that near-panicked place where she didn't feel complete without Frank at her side. Her lungs constricted and she demanded more of herself. She couldn't give in to these detrimental reactions or this frantic *need* to see him whole and hale.

When she'd identified his body, believing

herself a widow, she'd been calm. Not happy, not relieved, but calm. She had been devastated that he was gone—that he hadn't trusted her with whatever had been happening those last months of his life. But he had taken any decision or worry away from her. She had accepted that reality and tried to get on with her life. No more questions about whether or not he was okay, no more wondering if he would return, just a numb finality. Knowing he was alive and being unable to tell anyone presented the strangest paradox. Part of her wanted to celebrate, while an equally strong part of her wanted to shake him.

What would he do if she walked right on past their meeting point? Her knees trembled at the thought and she hurried toward the nearest open bench. As the owner of a security company, she employed the cream of the bodyguard crop. Frank had warned her of a threat. A logical woman would assign a protective detail. Surely with all the friends she had in this city, she could evade Halloran until her detail arrived.

Where would that leave Frank? Damn it. She couldn't leave him to cope with Halloran's schemes alone. If she left him hanging, Frankie would never forgive her. She'd never forgive herself. No matter that his decisions had hurt her so deeply, she couldn't do the same to him.

She glanced around once more, confirming she was alone, before pulling out her phone. No word from Frank. Refusing to give in to the panic, she sent a text message to Victoria canceling their shopping date. Then she sent another to Frankie explaining away the trip to DC as a business lead. Both women responded quickly, giving her a moment's peace. The next incoming message, filled with links to bridal websites, brought a smile to her face.

Sophia was drafting another message to Aidan, a not-so-veiled warning, when she looked up and recognized Frank's rapid, ground-eating stride. He looked well and he hadn't tried to shut her out after all.

Relief propelled her from the bench in a rush. She didn't care if they made a scene as she wrapped her arms around him and pressed up on her toes for a kiss. Looking startled, he seemed to need a second to catch up. When he did, the kiss ignited as they rediscovered sweet, familiar contact. The heat of his wide hands seeped through the soft fabric of her knit dress, chasing away the earlier chill of anxiety.

"I'm still mad at you," she said when they paused long enough to breathe. "And you're late."

"I can tell."

The sexy grin on his face disappeared and

he turned, keeping one hand locked around hers as they headed back to the parking garage. The rigid set of his shoulders and the lines bracketing his mouth were evidence enough that something unfortunate had happened while she was talking with her friend.

"How was your meeting?" he asked.

She glanced up at him. "There's good news and bad news. What happened to you?"

"I had an impromptu meeting." He seemed to scan and evaluate the people around them for any threat.

"Care to elaborate?" She was doing her best to keep up with his longer legs, but walking with Frank when he was in a rush always turned into a cardio workout.

"Not here."

She'd never seen him in such a paranoid state. Though he'd always been observant and aware, this hypervigilant attitude was now and clearly a by-product of the situation. It seemed cruel, on this gorgeous spring day, to be plagued by such dark circumstances.

"What happened, Frank?" she asked when they reached the privacy of the rental car.

"I saw a man tailing me. I led him away from you and took care of it."

Took care of it? She choked.

"Relax." His voice was tight, stern. "When did you start believing I'm a cold-blooded—"

"Stop." She couldn't let him finish. "I do *not* believe that. Who tailed you?"

"One of Hellfire's young guns."

"Was he sent to kill you?" Fear tightened around her chest.

"No." Frank sighed, seeming to calm down as he drove toward the Beltway. "He was nothing but a messenger. He mentioned the 'top brass' had filled my account with a comeback incentive. He also gave up a name I hadn't heard before—Engle. I think Hellfire might let each leader hire his own help. The kid made it sound as though he was working directly for this Engle person, though he understood it was a bigger operation."

"Okay." She pulled out her phone and started a basic search. "What else did he tell you?"

"He couldn't call off the pending hit on you or Frankie, though he implied everything would be fine if I started cooperating again."

"He didn't ask about the missing drugs?"

Frank shook his head. "That bugged me, too." He changed lanes, then reached into his jacket pocket. He set a cell phone and wallet in the cup holders between the seats. "I took those off the kid. Told him to turn himself in before I made it look like he flipped on Hellfire. That cut right through his bravado, even as he told me Engle wouldn't believe it."

She checked the ID in the wallet and did a cursory search of the cell phone. "We need to pull what we can from this immediately. Before he can wipe any data remotely."

"You can do that from here?"

She nodded, thinking Aidan would make short work of her request. "My assistant can pass it on to our internal security team."

"No." He checked his mirrors and changed lanes again. "I don't want to give Halloran any reason to move on Frankie or the company."

"Frank, we need them." When would he accept that? "The company we dreamed of is founded on discretion." Her mind leaped into overdrive as she scrolled through the young man's text message history. "If these contact numbers track to real accounts, this is a gold mine," she murmured, sending screenshots to her phone. "We have to verify right away."

"What about the friend you just met with of the Colby Agency? Can't either of them handle this?"

"I promise Frankie and Leo Solutions won't be tied to any of it. She's actually oblivious of any trouble. I just got a text with links to a site full of bouquet ideas."

"Wedding bouquets?"

"Yes. She's so excited—"

He silenced her with a stony look. "You've been texting her from a phone we know Halloran can track?"

She pressed her lips together, breathing slowly through her nose, reminding herself he had many valid reasons to be paranoid. "My GPS is deactivated," she said carefully. "You and I both know they're tracking me through other means. I'd no more put our daughter in danger than you would." She paused when her voice started to shake with renewed anger. "Why don't you take a minute, Frank, and decide once and for all? Either you trust me to help you wipe out Hellfire or you don't."

While she waited for his response, she used her phone to take pictures of the contents of the wallet. In addition to the driver's license and two credit cards, there was an employee badge from a company whose name she didn't recognize. These she sent to her friend Eddie here in DC.

"Do what you have to do," Frank muttered after what felt more like an hour than a minute. "I trust you."

"Thank you."

Sophia sent all the new information to her assistant, asking her to walk the information directly to Aidan. When the information was confirmed to have been received by her assistant, she turned off the young man's cell phone and tossed it and the wallet into her purse.

"Engle doesn't ring any bells for you?" Sophia asked as Frank started another loop around the city. "Where are we going?"

"I don't know yet," he admitted, adjusting his ball cap. "Tell me what you learned this morning." He turned a bit and one eyebrow lifted over his sunglasses. "Better yet, tell me who you met with."

"An old friend," she replied. As tightly wound as Frank was, the truth would only prove problematic.

"Come on, Sophia. I have a right to know. Was it an old CIA pal?"

Her temper flashed. She wanted to deny his right to everything, but he'd just promised to trust her and she couldn't give him reason not to now. "As far as anyone else is concerned, I met with a lawyer."

"Eddie Chandler?" His grip on the steering wheel tightened and his nostrils flared.

She leaned across the console. "You can't still be jealous. It's been over thirty years." There had been only one man in her past who had eroded Frank's confidence—her college boyfriend and first fiancé. She'd called off the engagement, met Frank within a year of her graduation and never looked back, yet something about that old relationship had always put Frank on edge and filled him with senseless worry.

She drilled her finger into his arm. "I married *you*." They had far bigger problems than his lingering jealousy.

"I knew it." Frank's eyebrows snapped together over his sunglasses. "Did he start in with that old crap about how you'd be better off without me?"

"That was always a joke. He got married ages ago, remember?"

Frank only grunted.

"And he can't warn me away from you, because I'm still a *widow* per public opinion."

"Knowing how my career imploded, he must have given you some variation of 'I told you so.'"

"Aside from a sincere expression of sympathy for my loss, your name didn't come up." She rubbed the base of her left ring finger, suddenly missing her wedding rings. "I walked in with one purpose—intel on Darren Lowry."

"Right." Frank muttered a nearly inaudible oath. "What did you tell him?"

"I let him assume my inquiry had something to do with Leo Solutions business. He remembered the complaint in Iraq. Naturally, we couldn't go through the official records, but Eddie knew of more than one complaint."

"Doesn't sound like much progress."

Sophia didn't correct her grumpy husband right away. Primarily what she'd wanted, what Eddie had provided, was a clean computer to do more research in the hopes of finding something they could use against Lowry. "I found his civilian résumé, and since I still have access to the archives within the CIA, I took some time and made notes of professional intersections between Lowry and Halloran. I was looking for the catalyst."

"Sophie." Frank groaned. "Might as well send up a flare."

She understood and forgave his dismay. He'd been in the thick of Hellfire longer, his life had been wrecked, and he'd been the whipping boy for Halloran's crimes. And he had no idea what she could do with a computer these days.

"We needed the information. The more we know, the more options we have." She barreled on when he started to disagree. "You warned me not to go at Halloran directly. I didn't. Unless this is far bigger than either of us can imagine, no one will even be aware of my search." To his credit, Frank gestured for her to go on.

"You have his current address and you know

Lowry works at the Pentagon as a defense contractor. I learned his current project is developing new, longer-lasting batteries for special forces units."

"How the hell did you and Eddie discover that?"

Sophia eyed Frank and decided to ignore his jealousy and to treat him as she would a moody, frustrated client. "Lowry and Halloran crossed paths plenty in their early careers. I couldn't identify a particular catalyst, though it's possible Halloran buried a few harassment complaints to get Lowry to go along with his plans."

"I doubt any threats were needed," Frank said. "Lowry is the sort who always keeps an eye open for the chance to make an easy buck. Half the time he sounded more like a shady stockbroker than an army officer."

That was precisely the information she needed from Frank to help them pry open Hellfire. "Is he the moneyman?" She couldn't imagine Halloran would be that foolish. "Why put a greedy personality type in charge of the money?"

Frank snorted. "Skills and deniability? Greed doesn't often come with self-control."

"From what you've said, the crew has been

greedy and successful in it for a long time."
How could they use that?

"You didn't run across anyone named Engle
in your research?"

"No." She decided not to pull out the papers
she'd printed for further analysis. That would
give Frank only more cause for concern. "Then
again, I wasn't looking for it."

"You can't go back to Eddie's office," Frank
said quickly. "We need to keep moving."

She understood the risks of staying in one
place long enough for Halloran to catch them,
but there had to be a way to take a swipe at
Lowry before they left. "Lowry is in town. We
could stay close for a day or two, pick apart
his life and find something to wave like a red
flag in front of the press. Or we could tip off
a reporter with a completely bogus story and
hope it starts a chain reaction."

"You tell me what you want," Frank said,
sounding surprisingly relaxed.

They definitely couldn't keep driving around
the Beltway. "I want a hotel with decent internet access and a few hours to see if I can find
the right buttons to push. I'm thinking we can
combine what we know and pin an information leak on the guy who tailed you today."

"Then we'll do that," said Frank. "There are

plenty of options near Reagan National Airport and we can scoot out of town right away."

The sooner the better, she thought. Eddie had suggested a reporter for Sophia to contact if they wanted the media to start prodding Halloran's operation. It was time to get aggressive. Frank had been going at this quietly and under the radar for a while, but he had backup now, whether he wanted it or not. What she had in mind would keep Halloran's mind off Frankie.

Thinking of her daughter reminded her about the bridal links. She clicked on them, did a fast cruise through the pictures and sent Frankie a reply.

"Did you think of something else?" Frank asked.

"Not yet. I was responding to Frankie's links."

Her husband paled visibly.

"Do you need to pull over? I can drive if you can't handle the idea of your baby getting married," she offered.

"I trust you." Frank seemed to have trouble swallowing. "I just—" He shook his head and clutched the wheel as a car cut him off.

Sophia stiffened, braced for another attack. None came, though she couldn't quite relax. Part of the problem was the tautness in every line of Frank's posture. "What is it?"

She glanced around, twisting in her seat as she tried to identify the threat.

"Nothing." He wasn't convincing. "It's the idea of Halloran getting a hold of Frankie. I believe you," he said quickly. "I *do*." He scrubbed at his jaw. "I just can't shake that image."

"Aidan won't let anything happen to her. I believe he'd be enough even if she wasn't surrounded by bodyguards."

"Yeah." Frank followed the signs for the airport.

"I think our daughter has skills we could use here, but I won't involve her in this unless we agree. I promise we're only trading wedding ideas by text message. It's what we do now." It still gave her a happy maternal thrill, but she was dealing with a dad who felt left out. Changing the subject, she asked, "What else did you learn from the guy who tailed you?"

Frank sighed. "He said Halloran hadn't intended to leave me in prison to serve out the treason charge."

"You're kidding."

"Not a bit. I guess Hellfire would've broken me out. Or that could've been the nice way of saying they would've killed me before I cracked."

He shifted restlessly in the seat until he had

his jacket off. The dark T-shirt emphasized his toned chest and arms, making her want to sigh.

"I made a lame offer to help him break free of Hellfire and he basically laughed in my face. Said if I was against Hellfire I was dead and he didn't want an outsider's help."

"Do you think they've brainwashed him?" That would put a new spin on the situation.

"No. I think he's a dark ops wannabe hungry for a bigger slice of the pie."

She didn't want to accept that Frank might be right about Hellfire being impossible to break. Every suit of armor had a weak spot. She just needed a bit of time to really take a look at Halloran's. She wouldn't accept failure here if for no other reason than to make sure Frankie and her father were reunited. "Where are we going?" she asked when he bypassed the airport and headed south.

"Alexandria. I changed my mind. I'd rather make the damned spies work for it if they want to retaliate. It's one of two rooms I booked earlier, just in case."

She recognized that tone. He'd dug in his heels and would be nearly impossible to budge. "Lowry has a meeting at the Pentagon tomorrow."

"How do you know that? Oh, never mind."

Frank rubbed his forehead. "You and Eddie planning to crash the meeting?"

She ignored that jab. "Alexandria is close enough."

"For what?"

"Well, if I can find something strong enough to use against him in the next few hours, I thought we might enjoy ringside seats for the media circus." She was thinking in particular of what Aidan could dig up. "His travel records for the past two years shouldn't be too hard to find and could give us some insight if we match them with dates and deposits. It's unlikely to be conclusive, but who knows what will break this case open?"

He didn't respond for a time and she chalked up his silence to traffic congestion and was lost in her own thoughts as they continued on to Alexandria.

"You and Eddie *are* planning something." His voice sounded weary with emotion.

"Yes." No sense denying it. She laced her fingers in her lap, determined to remain calm. "We're planning to clear your name and see the right people brought to justice."

He dropped the argument, though the resistance was evident in the muscle twitching in his jaw.

"Halloran and his cronies owe you and all

the people his crimes have affected," she continued. "I want bad publicity and disgrace to be part of his restitution."

"Because you were disgraced by me."

"The treason verdict and subsequent suicide weren't career highlights," she replied carefully. "It required a cautious walk over a bed of eggshells and nails to get Leo Solutions up and running. The company was the key to my future and Frankie's, too."

"I know. Now you and the company are tied to this mess. I should've insisted you go home to Frankie, surround yourself with bodyguards and sit this out."

"Once I knew you were alive, that was never going to happen. I'm not proud of the admission, but no one believed in you more than your daughter. I lost faith in you."

"You were right to lose faith in me. I don't want to hurt her any more than I already have. If something happens to you…" His voice trailed off.

She understood everything he couldn't quite articulate. "Although it might not be easy, we have to stick this out—together—for Frankie."

"She'll hate me for the lies and all the rest of it."

"I think you're underestimating her." Had he forgotten they'd raised their little girl to be a tough and determined woman who knew how to think for herself? "She'll forgive you in an instant."

His mouth twisted into a frown. "Next you'll want me to get on a video call and apologize to her."

"That's your business." She'd intended to say more but went mute as he pulled into a hotel where they'd stayed after a holiday party when they were newlyweds. "Frank, you didn't?"

"I didn't use my real name. Though it's tough to see the point in hiding. Halloran's spies will pick us up soon enough."

"Then why invite trouble to a place where we have such fond memories?" If this was an attempt to rekindle something, she didn't know how to feel about that. She thought of the kiss earlier. That had been her fault. Clearly the sizzling attraction between them hadn't completely faded. Still, after everything he'd had to do to survive and the choices she'd made as a widow, there was a new awkwardness she couldn't quite navigate.

"It's a hotel, Sophia. They had an opening and I booked it."

She didn't believe that for a minute.

Chapter Six

Frank watched Sophia carefully, searching for any insight to what was going on behind those stunning eyes. Maybe this had been a bad idea, indulging in an opportunity to revisit the fond memories of a holiday nearly thirty years past, but he was only human.

Once they were in the room, Sophia was all business. She wasted no time setting up her computer and starting in on her research. Frank didn't much care how they got Lowry, as long as they did something to show Halloran they weren't going to stop.

While Sophia picked apart Lowry's life, Frank went back through his notes, trying to connect the Engle name to the Hellfire puzzle. The more he thought about it, the more he felt he should know that name. He just couldn't place it.

Taking a break, he stood up and stretched

his legs, gazing around the luxurious room, wondering how his wife could be so unaffected by the memories assaulting him. She'd kissed him senseless earlier. Had it been for show, or was he a fool to think he'd felt a remnant of their old passion in her kiss? He understood the concept of her relegating him to the past in order to move forward. Broad concepts be damned, they were back together. They were in the same room for another night. Did she feel anything at all for him?

"Yes!" she cried, giving him a start. "Come take a look." She waved him over. "I've got the travel records." She gave him a sly look. "And I found some rather suggestive exchanges on his contractor email account."

He skimmed the highlighted passages long enough to realize the woman being propositioned wasn't amused by the idea. "What an idiot."

"For which we shall be grateful," she said. "He doesn't need or care about the job. It's little more than a cover."

Frank whistled at the implications. "Show me." He followed along as she explained the business travel records. "Whoa." Frank flipped open his notebook and they compared dates. "That lines up almost perfectly with the shipments I've tracked."

Her smile brightened the whole room. Her laptop keys clicked in rapid-fire succession. "I'm drafting an email to the CID now."

"Anonymous source?"

"Yes. It won't take much work to verify the facts we're providing. I'll copy Eddie, too."

She was so proud of herself. Hell, he was proud right along with her. He'd been working for months to find an angle and hadn't made this much progress. Striding to the window, he peeked through the edge of the curtain. They'd been here for over two hours and he was sure Halloran had to have someone on them by now.

Frank systematically picked apart everything within his view from the window. He'd chosen this hotel and asked for a room on this side for the view of the Potomac, the memories of better days and the stronger defense options. The way this end of the block was laid out, the hotel was hemmed in by the river and a park. It gave Frank a modified box-canyon trap that would allow him to escape safely with Sophia should they need to get away quickly.

"Did you hear me?"

Her question cut through his search for any menace lurking outside. Trying to relax, he smiled as he turned back to her. "I was thinking about other details."

Her dark brown gaze zeroed in on him. "You're expecting company?"

The intensity, her ability to see through any smoke screen was nearly more than he could bear. He shouldn't burden her with these overwhelming feelings right now. Survival first, and the rest would fall into place if it was meant to be or, rather, if she'd have him.

"No," he replied. "We're fine. What were you saying?" He caught the smirk on Sophia's face. He knew that look. "What did you do?"

That smirk turned into a wide, lovely smile. "At Eddie's office today, I took advantage of a computer that couldn't be traced and put a few things in motion while we did our research."

It made him wonder if the beatific smile was for him or her old friend. Didn't matter. Survival came first right now. "Not entrapment?"

"No. We agreed *neither* of us would break the law." Her emphasis served as a reminder to him, as well. He got the message loud and clear. "Although it's not entrapment, since we're not actually representing any branch of law enforcement."

"You know what I mean."

She grinned, unrepentant. "I sent copies of the sexual harassment article we found last night to the CEO of the defense contractor, a reporter Eddie recommended, as well as to a well-known feminist group. One of them is bound to follow up and make life difficult for him. Add in the travel records to places a little off the contractor's itinerary and I think we can call it a good day's work."

He closed his eyes and shook his head. Assuming she was right, that would stir the pot for sure.

"What? It's public record. I thought you'd be happy. If we're lucky, he'll be under some kind of investigation by tomorrow morning."

"Investigation is a lofty goal," Frank said, amused by her high hopes. He wouldn't be unhappy if it happened that fast.

She flicked her fingers, dismissing his cynicism. "He'll be in the news, that's the point."

"Halloran will be mad as hell." He turned back to the window, thankful one of them was making progress. It wasn't a bad system, him guarding her while she systematically dismantled the people he identified. It wasn't a real life, but it felt good to be working as a team again.

He heard the desk chair squeak as she stood. Although the carpet muffled the sound of her footsteps, he felt her crossing the room to stand at his shoulder. Lilies and spices teased his nose.

"Were we followed?"

"I can't be sure yet. With his assets, it's more than likely Halloran will track us down by nightfall." He felt the heat of her body all along his side as she leaned close to peer over his shoulder while dusk fell outside.

"Because we were together when you rented the car?"

"In his shoes, I'd track airport security cameras for your arrival, then follow along until you met up with me. It's the easiest way to catch us," he said, deciding it was better to be honest about everything.

"If he has the access, that's the right approach."

He glanced down at her, struck as he always was by how beautiful she was. In his opinion the crinkles of laugh lines at her eyes and the deeper lines in her forehead only made her lovelier. The face he'd fallen in love with, with more experience. Everything about her called to him, body, mind and soul. How had he screwed up their lives so badly?

Dropping the curtain, he turned fully, leaning against the windowsill to be closer to eye level. How many things he needed to say and couldn't. Not until he had a right to say them again. How badly he wanted to claim every benefit as her husband. Making a move right now would be disastrous. In the long run, moving too soon would be more disastrous than being framed for treason and forced to leave his family behind. If he confessed everything, asked forgiveness, and she walked away, he'd be broken beyond repair.

She cocked her head, studying him. "Should we go out on the town and party or hit the road and put hundreds of miles between where he thinks we are and where we're going?"

"No. We'll spend the night right here, within the safety of these walls." He wasn't sure he was talking about the case anymore.

"Frank." She folded her arms and rocked back on her heels.

"We'll keep at the research," he said, defending his decision. "We need to figure out who Engle is."

"Okay." She continued to stare him down.

"Would it make you feel better if I said it was too soon to be bait?" When her lips quirked to the side in amusement, he was tempted to steal a kiss as he'd done so often in the past.

"That helps a little." She sighed as she reached for the clip holding her hair up off her neck. "Research, it is. We're giving Lowry something to chew on, but it would be nice to take a swipe at the head honcho himself."

He was mesmerized with the way the sable locks spilled to her shoulders as she massaged her scalp, then piled it all back up again. He cleared his throat. "If Halloran's not playing golf in Arizona, he's doing something with the product or the profit. It's definitely too soon to go after him directly."

She rocked her head gently from side to side, stretching her neck, then frowned as a new thought hit her. "When was the last time you saw him in person?"

"Three months ago," he replied. "I watched him play a round of golf on an ocean-view course in Norfolk, Virginia."

Frank returned to his study of the area outside the hotel. Watching for Halloran's spies was far easier than watching her for signs that she might want to renew their relationship. She probably didn't want to waste any more romantic energy on him after what he'd put her through.

At least he'd booked a room with two beds tonight. No need for a debate as to who would sleep where this time around.

"It's a starting point," Sophia said quietly, not wanting to interfere with the quiet Frank seemed to need.

At the table, she toed off her shoes and drew up her legs, sitting cross-legged on the chair, the skirt of her dress pulled over her knees. She was suddenly cold and weary from one adrenaline rush after another for the better part of the past twenty-four hours. It didn't help that sleep had been sketchy at best last night.

It was difficult to focus on her search for Kelly Halloran when she kept staring at her husband as if she were sixteen again and hopelessly daydreaming about the hunky quarterback of the high school football team. She closed her laptop and picked up her phone, finishing that text she'd started for Aidan. Odds were low Hellfire specifically was on the radar in Europe even though drug trafficking and money laundering were global problems.

Restless, she checked her email, finally pinpointing the real trouble when her stomach rumbled. "We need to eat." She trusted Frank's instincts about lying low tonight. "Why don't I order room service?"

"Go ahead." He walked away from the window and stuffed his hands into his pockets. "I'm not hungry."

She'd heard that before and learned the hard way. Frank would forget about food while his mind worked on a problem; then he'd be famished at the first whiff of a savory scent. Regardless of his appetite, he needed to fuel up. She ordered with great care, being sure to bring in enough food and avoiding anything reminiscent of their stay here nearly thirty years ago. That had been champagne and a decadent snack after a fun night of holiday schmoozing with friends. It felt as though all those years flashed by in a blink. One minute they'd exchanged vows as newlyweds and the next they were moving their only child out of college.

She'd realized months ago that part of her would always love Frank. No matter how their marriage had ended, the lies before and after, it was clear her heart had never stopped loving him. While it would be nice to revisit the good times with her best friend, she kept her thoughts to herself. She wouldn't risk the heartache for either of them by cruising down memory lane only to wind up at the abrupt, unexpected ending when he faked his death.

Room service knocked on the door just as she started to ask Frank where he'd spent those first nights out of prison. With Torres, probably. What about after that? She wanted to know if he'd been grieving the loss as much as she and Frankie had.

She yanked her thoughts away from that crumbling edge of insanity. It wasn't her business. It didn't even matter. He was alive and they would all deal with the effects of that in good time. Frankie should know her dad was alive and well, but Sophia couldn't begin to explain it all by text. As confident as she was about their daughter's reaction to the news, she had to respect Frank's reluctance.

Truly, they both had too much to deal with already.

When Frank was out of sight, she opened the door. After the food was set up and the waiter gone, Frank emerged and they sat down to thick, hot roast beef and turkey sandwiches, a bowl of mixed salad greens and crispy home-made potato chips served with a tangy barbecue sauce for dipping.

He devoured the food as if he hadn't eaten in a week. Sophia managed to hide her smile behind her sandwich. Watching him demolish bite after bite, pausing occasionally for a long drink of iced tea, seemed to make the years and stress fall away. She felt warm all over remembering some of their more memorable meals. Cooking had always been a fun adventure for both of them.

"You know what surprised me the most about playing dead?" Frank twirled a chip in the bowl of tangy sauce between them.

Sophia set aside her fork, still loaded with a bite of salad, as a wave of uncertainty rolled through her belly. She wasn't sure she wanted to do this. Not when the food had been so comforting a moment earlier. "What's that?"

"How much I missed that little iron table set."

Her jaw dropped. He couldn't be serious. Did he know she had it on her front porch now? "You gave me all kinds of grief when I bought it."

"It was clunky and heavy." He popped another chip into his mouth. "I was thinking of the freight when we had to relocate."

"You were thinking of your back," she said, teasing him as he teased her. "I never made you move it once we decided where it would be in each place."

"And I'm thankful for that," he said with a wistful smile.

Her breath caught and her heart twisted a little in her chest, as if it was possible to dodge the sharp blades of pain for what they'd both lost. "We shared a lot over that table." They'd picked it up when Frankie was about three and it had served them well in every home after.

"Even when I was deployed or traveling, I missed that table."

"You never said a word about it."

His ears were turning pink, an outward signal that the admission embarrassed him. "We all take for granted things that we shouldn't."

Was that some vague reference to her? She bit back the question. Dumb to think it, dumber to ask. "True." She couldn't understand when he'd thought anything was too silly or small to share with her. For twenty-eight years they'd been as close as two people could be. Then he'd pulled away until that little gap was insurmountable.

"We shared a lot over that table," she said. "Coffee on Sunday mornings was the best."

"I was partial to the late evenings after Frankie had gone to bed," he said, a twinkle in his dark blue eyes.

Those had been wonderful evenings, with beer or wine, stargazing or people-watching while they held hands. When the little table set had been in a more private area, she'd often been convinced to sit in his lap and make out under the stars.

Was this her estranged husband's way of hitting on her? She found it more appealing than she should. "Those were good times, too," she admitted, pleased her voice was steady. Those nights bore a striking resemblance to this one: alone, sharing food and conversation across a small table. If he invited her to sit in his lap, she'd have a fight on her hands to remember how to say no. Her body temperature seemed to climb at the very idea, heating her cheeks so he'd know exactly where her thoughts had traveled.

"Assuming your email campaign keeps Lowry busy, we need to think about Engle, Farrell and the next step," he said, leaning back in his chair.

The abrupt change of topic and the shift in his body language as he returned to business gave her a chill. It was as though he'd flipped a switch and all that intimacy had been in her imagination. "Farrell?" She picked up a chip. "Is he the third anchorman for Hellfire?"

Frank nodded.

"Why do I know that name?" She was excellent with names and yet she couldn't put a face with it at all. Probably because the face she was most concerned with was sitting right across the table, scowling fiercely. "Don't leave me hanging." She gestured for him to hurry up with the story.

"Jack Farrell is a retired colonel. He was career military police and honored as a hero when he shot a terrorist who managed to open fire on a forward operating base in Afghanistan a few years back."

Frank didn't have to say another word. She pressed her fingers to her lips as the scene, the reports, all of it surged through her mind with the force of a flash flood. "You don't think it was a terrorist."

He shook his head. "Not in light of what we know now. I think that attack was related to the early days of Halloran's effort to take his piece of the drug trade."

"Good grief. If only we could prove it," she mused, knowing they couldn't. "Halloran's assembled quite a team."

"Yes." Frank leaned back in the chair, his eyes on the ceiling. "Speaking of names to know, I sifted through the old reports and my notes looking for Engle while you were putting the finishing touches on ruining Lowry's reputation. I'm coming up empty."

Her cell phone chimed and she held up a finger. "Hold that thought." She read the message from her assistant, an update on the data they had pulled from the cell phone Frank confiscated earlier. "Pay dirt," she said.

"Tell me. We need good news."

She read the message and related the pertinent details. "My assistant identified the logo on that employee badge along with phone numbers in his text message history. They match up with an import-export brokerage."

She clicked the link in the email to go to the company website. "Oh! Look at this." She hopped out of her chair to kneel at his side so they could look at the small screen together. "I found Engle. He's listed as the operating manager at World Crossing, Incorporated."

Frank squinted at the phone screen. "Stateside offices in Norfolk and Seattle. The man doesn't lack for courage." He took the phone and swiped through the pictures. "Check the logo on the truck." He opened his notebook and showed her. "That's the freight carrier they use with every incoming shipment."

"I can use this." She bounded to her feet and retrieved her laptop.

"I've been an idiot," Frank said. "I should've known he would control every aspect."

Sophia sent an email to the reporter Eddie recommended, complete with the screenshots from the kid's phone. "I hope he took your advice," she murmured as she hit Send. "When this breaks, it will send Hellfire scrambling. If they don't believe him…"

"He made his choices," Frank said, his voice cold. "The more I think about Farrell, the happier I am that we'll have a head start." His gaze drifted toward the window. "Such as it is."

"They can't move on us tonight." She shrugged at his quizzical glance. "One look out that window and I knew why you'd booked this room. They'd have to scale the wall to get in."

"Or use the main door in the lobby."

"Please. I heard the false name you gave at registration." She wasn't going to fuel his worry. "Halloran's spies might find the car, but they won't figure out the room number before we check out."

He gave her the look she'd laughed at through the years. The twist of his mouth and crinkle at his eye that said he knew she was right but she'd never get him to say the words. Afraid of the happy little skip in her pulse, she returned to the task of digging into the lives of the men who'd founded this dangerous operation and turned their lives upside down.

Frank pushed the room service cart out to the hallway and stretched out on one of the beds, reading glasses perched on his nose as he studied his notebook.

It reminded her they had only days until a new shipment arrived in Seattle. If only Frank would agree, she could put a team on the ports. They needed a smaller target than "the waterfront." And she knew he was right to fear for Frankie's safety if Halloran or anyone else spotted a Leo Solutions team. Although her guys were good, it wasn't worth the risk. Yet.

"Huh. The only thing current on Jack Farrell is a PO box in Arizona." She tried a few more searches with no luck.

"Don't forget the bank account in the Caymans," Frank quipped. He sat up and lowered his reading glasses. "Wait. Phoenix?"

"No. Vail, Arizona. South of Tucson." She used the internet to pull up a local map. When Frankie was led to believe the worst about Sophia, the trail had taken her through a nearby area. She didn't care for the direction her thoughts were taking.

Following the hunch, she found another, unpleasant connection. "Paul Sterling went to college with Farrell, both political science majors," she told Frank. "And Farrell and Halloran attended the war college in the same year. It might be worth asking Paul about Farrell."

Frank's blue eyes were as cold as ice chips.

"For the record, asking Paul for help isn't my first choice," she stated.

"Visiting a prison isn't mine." Frank tapped his glasses against his thigh, his mouth twitching. "How'd you manage to get Sterling behind bars so fast?"

"You don't know what happened?"

He shook his head.

She didn't want to revisit all the details. "He fooled me, let's leave it at that. While he was in custody in Seattle, I reached out to an old friend inside the Department of Justice. Leo Solutions has a modest government contract arrangement. It wasn't much, but I was thankful they got him transferred to the federal prison in Maryland while he awaits trial."

"I don't think he'll want to cooperate with you after that."

"Us. If we do this, we do it together."

Frank sat up. "You're kidding. I can't walk into a prison, Sophie. Even if I wasn't recognized immediately, Paul would make a scene out of spite. He always hated me because I had you."

"The two of you were always competitive." When she thought she'd been widowed and needed help, Paul had been there for the business and, after a time, on a more personal level. Thinking of him, of how he'd deceived her so thoroughly, left her wanting a shower.

Frank stretched out again. "All the more reason not to trust anything he might tell us."

She held her tongue. Frank knew as well as she did they couldn't allow any part of Halloran's organization to escape justice. They had to nail all the top players or Frank would never have his life back. "We can't let Farrell off the hook because we can't find him. What we need is something to hand to a prosecutor. Paul could give us that kind of lead."

Frank shook his head and went back to his notebook.

The prison was a short drive and couldn't

possibly be on Halloran's radar. There was a regional airport close by where they could park the car and further hide their trail. It would become a pointless exercise if Frank got detained in the process.

She could ask him to wait with the car, but she couldn't bear it, not after her near panic attack in DC. "If I can guarantee you won't be detained, will you think about it?"

"It's a bad idea."

"I know that." Exasperated, she went over and sat on the edge of the bed, leaving as much space as possible between them. "I know there are better ideas. Do we really have the time for any of them? Your fake ID will work." He was shaking his head already. "I need you with me," she blurted. "I mean it, Frank. I'm not letting you out of my sight. My heart can't take the worry." She felt her heart pounding now, terrified if he left her sight that he'd be gone again. "I—I had anxiety attacks when we were younger. Wh-when—" she gulped "—when you were gone. In the beginning. Today when I thought you were gone…"

"Dolcezza," he whispered, reaching for her.

She dodged his hand, scrambling off the bed. If he touched her now, she wouldn't be able to resist him. Sex would only make things worse, blurring the lines and insinuating obligations she didn't want to push on him. If they could clear his name, maybe they had a shot at rediscovering their dreams as a couple, as a family. "I worked past those fears. I managed." She sucked in another breath. "Just not now." She rested her hand over her heart, willing it to slow down. "Come with me. Please."

"Of course."

Relief so profound she swayed with the force of it had her dashing for the bathroom. She splashed water on her face. She was grateful for not crying, though her face was a splotchy mess anyway. Her life was a mess.

Going to the prison to speak with Paul was a long shot. Even if he cooperated and shared what he knew about Farrell, spending a minute in his presence would be difficult enough. If he chose to be a jerk... Oh, it didn't bear thinking about.

She hadn't jumped into bed with Paul immediately following Frank's graveside service, yet trying to explain to her very alive husband that, after a time, she had done exactly that was not a pleasant prospect. She had been entirely fooled by Paul. And Frank.

At last her temper surfaced, saving her from a night of hiding in the bathroom wallowing in what-ifs and what-might-have-beens. She returned to the room and picked up her laptop, ready to review the best way to and from the prison, and how to keep Frank safe in the process. There were still plenty of people who owed her favors and she was ready to cash them in so her daughter could see her dad and they could all decide what came next.

Frank's strong hands landed on her shoulders, radiating warmth. Was she imagining any forgiveness in his touch? Did she want or need that forgiveness? She let him massage the muscles at her neck and shoulders, still aching after the recent attack.

"I've pulled myself together," she said.

"You always do."

"Paul helped me get Leo Solutions off the ground when I needed to move fast," she explained, latching on to the one point she didn't regret. By all accounts, she'd been a widow, personally and professionally. She never would have been able to establish Leo Solutions so efficiently or make the company relevant so quickly without Paul's help. He'd done that much right. Mostly. The bastard.

"To separate yourself from my problems?"

"Yes." She stated the fact calmly, her eyes locked on her monitor. "If the situation were reversed, I would've expected you to do the same thing. It was a future we had planned. A legacy we would leave for our daughter."

He came around to sit across from her, and something deep in his blue eyes contradicted her assessment. His scent surrounded her, and her muscles were loose and warm from his hands. "Frankie was injured, her navy career over." The memory of their daughter in that hospital room surrounded by the equipment and dire prognosis still haunted her. "She was too stubborn to accept any physical limits, then too angry with me for what she assumed was my blithely moving on without you."

She'd gone through all that alone. Frank had been overseas or in custody, unable to help.

"You both succeeded, despite all of it," he said.

Her temper crackled to life again. "Do you think I'm looking for your approval here?"

"No." He held his ground, typical Frank. "But you have it."

She stifled the hateful words that wanted to pour out and burn him as effectively as acid. He hadn't been a traitor, and, knowing that, she couldn't keep blaming him for what was done. They had to find their way forward from here. She had to help him extricate himself from Halloran's schemes.

For Frankie, if no one else. Her daughter needed her father and it was clear to Sophia that the opposite was equally true. Despite the pain his choices had caused, she couldn't let this opportunity to salvage the father-daughter relationship slip away. She hugged her arms around her waist. Frankie had been right all along; her belief had never faltered. Sophia couldn't say the same thing. Even now, understanding his impossible choices, she couldn't quite get past the residual frustration—with herself for giving up on him and with him for heaping sorrow on Frankie's life at the worst possible time.

"Sophie." He lifted the laptop away and cradled her hand, stroking gently along the bones of her wrist, to her elbow and then down to each finger.

Soothing and comforting. Her hand and arm melted at the familiar comfort and her heart followed suit. Here was what she'd been missing, what she'd longed for. Every deployment or career task that kept them apart, they'd had this to come home to: the steady, nurturing support they'd consistently found in each other.

She had considered herself an independent person for the entirety of their marriage. Sharing the burdens and joys of life didn't lessen any part of her or him as individuals. The camaraderie, the acceptance and easy affection, she hadn't known how much she depended on those intangible traits until they had been ripped from her life.

He murmured her name, his gaze full of such raw compassion she knew his thoughts mirrored her own. Slowly, he tipped up her chin. Slower still, giving her plenty of time and space to turn away, he lowered his mouth until his lips brushed softly across hers.

She welcomed his kiss, let it sink into her being. The immediate flash of heat and passion was as reassuring and familiar as everything else about him. This kiss was loaded with more tenderness, more patience than the one she'd planted on him in DC. She raked her fingers through his hair, angling her mouth for deeper access to all that she craved from him.

On a soft sigh, her lips parted. She relished the hot velvet stroke of his tongue over hers. His taste ignited her body in ways she hadn't let herself remember for the sole purpose of preserving her sanity. His palms smoothed over her shoulders, down her back and over the curve of her hips. Fingers flexed and teased, playing her body as though they'd never been parted.

Every reunion had been this way. Sweet and hot, they fell on each other with the pent-up longing distance had created. Her fingers knew the curve of his jaw, the small scar at his hairline. She knew just where to kiss his throat and make him shiver with anticipation.

Her hips flexed into him automatically, and the feel of his erection sent goose bumps racing over her skin. Her body was more than willing to make up for lost time. He could have her. She knew the pleasure she'd enjoy taking him deep inside.

For too long, she'd believed this depth of yearning and fulfillment was out of her reach. She'd spent so many terrible nights regretting every moment they hadn't seized because they'd been so sure they had plenty of time.

On a surge of need she pressed up on her toes and fused her mouth to his. Her husband, the love of her life and her soul mate, was right where he belonged at last. People didn't get second chances as precious as this one. She wouldn't squander it.

He boosted her up and she wound her arms and legs around him, troubles burned away by this glorious contact. The scruff on his jaw rasped against the fragile skin just under her ear as he murmured those delicious Italian endearments between nips of his teeth and soft kisses.

Somewhere in the back of her mind, she heard her daughter's false irritation imploring them to get a room. The memory was as effective as a bucket of ice.

"Stop." She bent her head, keeping her lips out of his reach. "It's not so simple." It took more effort than she expected to put her feet on the floor and remain steady.

"Not simple at all," he agreed, his arms still banded around her, holding her close to the marvelous heat and strength of his body.

She forced her palms flat against his chest, pushing just hard enough to back away. She inhaled, drawing in the first deep breath of air not entirely infused with his masculine scent.

Better. And a thousand times worse. "Guess we've still got it," she remarked, wishing it wasn't true. This powerful attraction complicated everything.

"Feels that way."

"For everyone's sake we, um, should..." She licked her lips, tasting him. "Uh, we should stick to the matter of clearing your name."

"Sophia?"

She looked away. "Don't try to get around me with those eyes and that tone. I can't pretend the past year didn't happen, Frank."

"I don't blame you for *any* of your choices."

She wished she could say the same. She shouldn't blame him—he'd been caught in a precarious dilemma—yet she did. Being disappointed in him when he'd been in such a dilemma added guilt to the rest of the churning mix in her gut. Holding her arm out as if it might be enough of a deterrent, she kept herself just beyond his reach.

"I appreciate that." She wasn't sure she deserved his understanding. Grabbing her toiletry bag, she headed for the bathroom, pausing in the doorway. The words scraped her throat raw as she pushed them out. "But I blame you for yours."

There, she'd said it. Now they both knew how awful she was.

His nostrils flared on a sharp inhale and his gaze shuttered as she closed the door between them.

Chapter Seven

At the regional airport, Frank parked the rental car in the hourly lot. He didn't expect the meeting with Paul to take long. They'd stowed their luggage in a locker near the restrooms and now were waiting for a cab to take them to the prison in Cumberland.

With little to occupy his mind, he congratulated himself on surviving another long night with his wife well out of his reach. Her breakdown, admitting she'd suffered so much anxiety over him in the early years, nearly crushed him. He admired her even more for overcoming it and, given a chance, he'd hold her close—as if a hug now would soothe away her old troubles.

The idea of holding her brought him right

back to the spectacular kiss that had put his world to rights again despite stopping far short of his body's ultimate goal. He understood why Sophia had pulled away and couldn't resent her for it. He'd broken the most essential promise—to always be there for her.

He'd abused her trust. She wasn't sure she could count on him anymore. As messed up as things were with Halloran's operation, Frank maintained a fair confidence that they could bring that man and his cronies to justice. But the trust issue, the gaping canyon between husband and wife—that he wasn't so sure could be resolved.

"Breaking news." Sophia nudged him with her elbow and raised her chin at the television mounted in the corner of the tiny coffee shop.

In slacks and a classic sweater set in a pale rose color that put a glow in her golden skin, she looked overdressed for a trip to a prison. Having spent some time on the wrong side of the bars, he knew he was overdressed, as well. He'd chosen khakis and a polo shirt, hoping the guards would believe his impersonation of a lawyer taking a break between the front nine and back nine.

"Hey." She bumped him again. "You're not paying attention."

This time when he glanced at the television,

he read the ticker. The overhead shot of the Pentagon on this sunny spring day was layered with a professional head shot of Lowry. When the live feed returned, it was a view of Lowry being led out of the building in handcuffs toward a black government-issue sedan.

"Nice work," he murmured, though no one was around to hear him. Lowry in official custody would definitely get a rise out of Halloran. Frank was more eager for the next confrontation than he should be. He wanted the leader of Hellfire to understand, to absolutely *fear*, what Frank and Sophia planned to dish out. Justice, yes, along with enough pain to qualify as vengeance.

"It may not hold him long, but it should get a reaction. The intel from the phone gave my earlier claims more juice," she said. She held up her hand for a celebratory fist bump.

Preferring a kiss, he understood the line she'd drawn. "We're dealing with some cool heads," he reminded her. Halloran hadn't created his network and cash cow by jumping at every little provocation. Then again, the provocation Sophia had created wasn't so little.

"We're also dealing with egos and profit margins," she returned. "I doubt Lowry will roll on his boss. We just need to cast doubts."

"Regardless, this distraction buys us time to

question Paul and move before they can catch up with us."

Beside him, she nodded and crossed her legs. "Anyone here of concern to you?" she asked.

"Not so far."

"Good."

"You seem nervous." He wanted her to share the cause of her antsy behavior. More, he wanted her to trust him to help her fix it.

"I expected them to follow us."

"They'll catch up soon enough," he said. "Are you spoiling for a fight?"

"I suppose," she admitted. "It would be nice to have a clear target for all my frustration."

"Your frustration or your company?"

"The company resources there would give us an advantage." She checked her watch, then the window. "I thought cabdrivers stuck close to airports."

"If we tap the company, we put people we love in the cross fire."

She rolled her lips between her teeth and then gave him a wide, false smile. "We'll table the topic for now. Let's review the interview strategy."

They'd done that for most of the two-hour drive. "We don't have to quiz Sterling at all." He couldn't decide if he wanted her to take him up on that offer or not. A small part of him wanted to gloat that Sophia was with him, again. Except he wasn't sure he'd get to keep her this time. "With Lowry in custody, I'm sure Farrell will show up."

"Do you know where?" She waited expectantly, but he didn't have an answer. "Unless we use other resources, we need the inside line on Farrell that Paul may be able to give us."

The implication was clear enough. Leo Solutions could run everything, if only Frank would agree. He wouldn't take the chance with Frankie's safety. It bothered him enough what Sophia had run through her assistant and that his girls were texting about wedding plans.

"You know, I could always talk to him alone."

"No," she replied a little too quickly. "If we're both there, he can't play either one of us."

"Okay." She was right, though he wondered how long it had taken her to come up with the argument. What he knew about Afghanistan and what Sophia had pieced together afterward would be a system of checks and balances if Paul tried to lie.

"There's our ride," he said as a yellow cab came into view. With his hand at the small of her back, he escorted her outside and into the waiting vehicle.

Sophia slid across the crackled leather seat of the old cab and gave the driver the address of the prison. She took a snapshot of the cabdriver's license on his dash and then entered a text message.

Frank raised an eyebrow in query.

"A precaution," she replied quietly. "My assistant knows I'm on a research trip for a client."

He nodded, unable to come up with a response that wouldn't reveal the turmoil inside him.

They didn't speak to each other or the driver. The vehicle hadn't been upgraded with a screen between the front and back seats, and there wasn't much worth discussing in front of a stranger.

The reached their destination too soon. The driver could've taken all day and the trip would still have been too short for Frank. When they arrived, he got out and held the door for her before giving the cabdriver a hundred dollars in cash to wait for them. When it was time to go, he wanted to get out fast.

If walking into a prison on nothing more than her word that he wouldn't have to stay indefinitely didn't prove how much he trusted her, he wasn't sure what would.

"I know this can't be easy," she said, linking her hand with his.

"I'm fine," he lied through gritted teeth. He couldn't let her know just how much he wanted to run. It wasn't about seeing the bastard who'd taken advantage of her in Frank's absence. He'd had time to process that she'd run to Sterling for help after the verdict and funeral. It was about being trapped and never being able to be with her and their daughter the way he wanted.

Her steps slowed as they neared the gate. "Frank?"

Behind the shelter of his sunglasses, he studied her with unveiled love until his face felt normal again. "A half hour is worth it for a decent lead on hard intel."

Surely his fake ID and the myriad favors people owed Sophia would protect them that long.

SOPHIA FELT TERRIBLE for asking Frank to take this chance, but she couldn't risk leaving him back at the hotel area waiting somewhere between here and there. Not to mention, she couldn't face Paul alone. The tendons and muscles of Frank's hand were wound tight, and when she slipped her finger to his wrist, she felt his pulse pounding. He was doing a good job at being stoic and supportive, letting none of the stress show.

She'd cleared the visit early this morning and as they passed through security, the guard told them Paul was waiting. Good. She wanted in and out of here as quickly as possible.

As much as she tried to ignore the awkwardness, it dogged her as she and Frank walked down the faded, industrial-green hallway to a conference room. She was about to stand with her husband and interview a lover who'd betrayed her. If there had been a stranger situation in her past, she couldn't recall it right now.

Her heart hammered in her ears and she tried to imagine the best possible outcome. Though Paul might try to expose Frank's true identity, he wouldn't once he learned about the proverbial ace she had up her sleeve. Still, the potential for such a confrontation put an electric current in the air. The mocking expression she'd come to hate slid over Paul's face the second he spotted them. She raised her chin, entering the room first, daring him to try something. After the havoc he'd created for her and the company in Seattle, he owed her a conversation.

The metal chairs scraped loudly against the concrete floor as Frank pulled out hers, then his own. Paul's handcuffs rattled as he shifted in his seat. "What a pleasant surprise for me this morning."

"We're here for one thing." Sophia wouldn't waste any time on false pleasantries.

Paul's mean gaze darted between her and Frank. "Does that go for the dead guy, too?"

She glanced down and noticed Frank's hand curling into a fist on his thigh. She didn't blame him. Given the chance, she'd happily deck Paul, as well. "You went to college with Jack Farrell. Tell me about him."

Paul's eyebrows climbed his forehead. "Farrell." His eyes slid to Frank again. "Huh. If I knew anything, why would I tell you?"

Sophia cleared her throat, drawing Paul's attention. "You told me you didn't have anything to do with Frank's career troubles, that you only took advantage after the fact."

He gave her a lecherous sneer. "You didn't have any complaints at the time."

Frank shifted in a blink and the table was suddenly pressed against Paul's chest. "What did they offer you to get close to her?"

It seemed she and Frank had independently reached a similar conclusion overnight after discovering the import-export office in Seattle. As a friend, Farrell could have used Paul to be sure Sophia and Frankie weren't uncovering anything that would expose Hellfire.

"She came to me," Paul grumbled.

"Enough," Sophia said quickly. She pulled the table back to neutral territory. "I've been going through the company records. Seems you knocked some sense into me last week."

"What?" Frank asked, his voice low and deadly.

She silenced him with a touch of her knee to his. "Water under the bridge." She focused on Paul again. "I came to you for help, yes. When did Farrell come to you?"

"He wanted a cybersecurity program. We needed clients." He shrugged. "Later they tossed me a bonus to keep an eye on you and your girl. Money wasn't the best prize." His gaze dropped to her breasts and climbed slowly back to her face.

Her blood curdled at the vulgar look on his face. How had she been so oblivious of his real motives? "Tell me about Farrell and the program he asked for."

"Why? It's not as though you'll make my life any better."

"I bet she can make it worse," Frank threatened. "Or I can."

"You think a dead man scares me?"

"Hey!" Sophia rapped her knuckles on the table. Time to lay out all the cards. "I've been digging, Paul." Money was the man's only priority and she'd found his stash. "That makes *me* the real threat here." Since his arrest, she'd changed his passwords and her tech team had rooted out all his backdoor access to Leo Solutions. One call and Paul would find the money he was counting on using after his time served had been donated to the charity of her choice. She waited, holding his gaze as his skin blanched. "Are we on the same page now?"

Paul nodded solemnly, fear in his eyes for the first time.

"I'm determined to set the record straight," Sophia said. "I can see that you get lumped in with the rest of them, or I can tell the prosecutors that your connection to General Leone's downfall was peripheral. You have fifteen minutes to convince me the latter is our best interest."

With a heavy sigh, Paul shared everything he knew about his college pal. From Farrell's upbringing to the current business interests Paul was aware of.

"Where is he now?" Sophia asked, making notes.

"Last I heard he splits his time between his place south of Tucson and a desk in some accounts receivable department," Paul replied.

"Tucson," she echoed. Paul had planted documents in a safe-deposit box in a bank near Tucson, using the find to manipulate Frankie.

"There's a reason I used that bank." His mouth curved into an ugly smile, confirming he'd read her mind. "Image is everything, isn't it? Especially when the culprit is right under your nose."

Her teeth clenched. "Be clear," she insisted. Frank's future was riding on this.

"World Bridge Shipping, maybe?" Paul's brow wrinkled in thought. "Something like that. I know there's more than one office in the States," he added. "Farrell doesn't do anything for the money. Doesn't need it. He's got a warped thing for power and respect." Paul shook his head. "If you want him, try Arizona." He flattened one hand over the other and leaned forward. "I gave you all you need. I expect you to do the same."

She nodded. Paul was all about the money. The man had her tense from her scalp to the soles of her feet. As much as she hated this meeting, it gave them a fresh lead angle to pursue. She wouldn't rest until the right man— or men—was behind bars for the crimes he'd pinned on her husband.

"Thank you for your time," she said, sliding out of the seat.

Neither man moved, locked in a silent battle

of wills. "Don't you dare make a scene," she said, not certain which man worried her more.

"It was a pleasure seeing you again," Frank said, his chair scraping obnoxiously against the floor. "I look forward to the next time."

Only a deaf woman would've missed the threat in those words.

"Can't wait," Paul muttered before calling for the guard.

Though Paul had been her ally through the years, she knew she'd never speak to him directly again. It startled her how what appeared to be the smallest decisions could have such lasting, enormous impact. Frank had withdrawn from her to attend to an honorable task, willing to endure erroneous accusations for the betterment of his country. Paul had been attentive, heedless of her feelings while he deceived her day in and day out.

Sophia wasn't sure Victoria had been right about her judgment after all.

When the last heavy door rolled back and the sunshine blasted them, Frank swore. "We're stranded."

Startled, she searched the parking area as if she could will the cab to reappear. Thank goodness they'd left their belongings in a locker at the airport. "His dispatcher must have called him back."

"Not likely," Frank mused, donning his sunglasses. "This stinks of trouble."

She pulled out her phone and called the cab company. No answer. "Considering what we paid the driver to stay, it must have cost them a pretty sum to get him to leave."

"Not much comfort in that." He planted his hands on his hips, his mouth set in a stern line.

His eyes hidden, she couldn't see his gaze roaming over the area, but she knew he was searching for the inevitable ambush.

"Get back inside," he said, pushing her behind him. "I've got a bad feeling."

"What?" How was she supposed to manage that? It wasn't a restaurant or a salon—it was a federal prison. "I'm not going anywhere without you."

"By now Paul's telling them who I really am. You need to distance yourself."

She heard the unspoken *again*. "No." Had he forgotten how stubborn she was? "Paul will keep his mouth shut."

He pushed up his sunglasses, and his eyes were blazing. "What do you have on him?"

She gave him her sweetest smile. "About seventeen million dollars."

Either Frank didn't believe that would be enough incentive or he didn't care. "We've been set up, Sophie," he said, covering his eyes again. "Inside is your best chance."

Behind her own sunglasses, she studied the front gate, the towers and the cleared terrain outside the tall fences topped with barbed wire. She and Frank wouldn't be able to outrun an ambush. "A rock and a hard place," she murmured. They needed a car.

"Go on. They'll let you in."

She ignored him. Arguing wouldn't solve their dilemma. "The private ride apps won't do us any more good than the cab at this point. Too rural."

"There's no cover." His voice was little more than a growl as he started to walk.

Sophia followed. She had an overhead image of the area on her phone. "There's a farm three miles down the road," she said. "If we can get there, we can—"

"They'll pick us off long before either of us can get there," he said. He stopped pacing in front of the warden's vehicle parked at the front of the lot and urged her to join him. "Let's see how determined they are."

The grit in his voice gave her a boost of confidence. "What do you mean?"

"I'm waiting right here." He sat down on the curb, his hands resting on one knee, his other leg stretched out long. "They'll get impatient and make a move or we'll find another ride out of here."

"It is a nice day to sit outside," she said, playing along. At least he wasn't implying they steal a car from in front of a prison. "All we're missing is a picnic."

He tilted his head up to her, his lips curved in a genuine smile. If she didn't know better, she'd say he looked happy.

"I've missed that," he said.

"What?"

"Your wit," he replied. "Your unflappable nature."

"Both are essential survival skills in our worlds."

"I agree." He scanned the parking lot once more.

"You're using the reflection in the windshields to check behind us, aren't you?"

"Surprising what skills you pick up when you're on the run."

She sat down beside him and tried to call the cab company again. "How can they just not answer?"

Frank shrugged. "Halloran plays a ruthless game."

"And you?"

"I've learned to play that way when there's no other choice."

She left that comment alone, sending a quick text to Leo Solutions. Frankie or Aidan would figure it out if something happened to her. She had yet to explain anything other than that she was running down leads for an old friend. Frankie would flip out, temper blazing, if she discovered her dad was alive and avoiding her.

"What are you thinking?" she asked after a few more minutes of silence.

"Time is on our side. Coming directly at us would cause them more problems than it solves. Walking to the farmhouse is iffy, gives the advantage back to them. Between the two of us I'm sure we can convince one of the deliverymen to give us a lift out of here."

"Putting that driver in jeopardy."

"Face it, Sophia—anyone near us right now is in jeopardy. That doesn't make us the bad guys."

True. She just didn't want to see anyone else get hurt.

"Do you believe Sterling?"

"Yes." She pulled up the regional airport, checking departures. "Do you think we'll get lucky and pin down Farrell in Tucson?"

"Until Halloran shows his lousy face, it's our best option." Frank stood up at the sound of an approaching engine. "Well, well," he said. "Look who has a conscience."

Sophia noticed the number on the top of the yellow taxicab pulling into the lot. "It's the same car." She squinted but couldn't identify the driver through the glare on the windshield. "Is it the same driver?"

"Can't tell yet. Stay alert," he warned, walking out from between parked cars. "Could be a setup."

The cab came to a stop and the driver, the same man who'd brought them to the prison, stepped out. "I went to fill up the tank. Hope you haven't been waiting long."

"Thought you might've changed your mind about the fare," Frank said, opening the closest rear door for Sophia.

"No, sir. My apologies for any confusion."

"Back to the airport," Frank responded. He laced his fingers with hers, their joined hands resting on his thigh, his smile a hard counterpoint to the gentle touch.

She understood the unspoken message that he now considered the cabdriver an enemy until proved an ally. Hopefully he could still read her well enough to know she agreed.

They'd barely made the main road when she heard the growl of a burly engine speeding up behind them. Frank twisted in the seat, his eyebrows dropping into a ferocious scowl at the car closing in on the rear bumper of the cab.

"Get down," Frank said, urging her to the floorboards behind the driver's seat. "I guess they're convinced you could make Paul talk."

"They aren't wrong," she pointed out.

Frank leaned across the back of the front seat. "Any weapons?" he asked.

"No, sir."

Frank swore and her stomach clutched. They'd left Frank's weapons behind in the luggage. Assuming Halloran's men were armed and their intent was to stop her and Frank permanently, they were sitting ducks.

The car behind them slammed into the back of the cab. The impact knocked the cab forward with a hard jerk and tossed Sophia into the hard frame of the driver's seat.

"Floor it," Frank ordered.

When the driver obeyed, Sophia put him in the ally column and said a prayer all three of them would survive. The cab took another hit, this time closer to the right rear quarter panel. They were being pushed into the oncoming traffic lane and the driver eased off the gas.

"I'll pull over," the driver said.

"Do that and we're all dead," Frank snapped. "These people don't leave witnesses."

"Do you?" the driver asked.

Sophia lurched upright from her sheltered position. "Yes! Get us back to the airport in one piece and I'll make sure you can buy a new cab."

"You can do that?"

Under her feet she felt the cab accelerating again. "Yes!" she answered. "I can make sure you have money to put your kids through college or whatever you need."

The driver's eyes lit up and the heavy cab sped up a little more. "You are good people. College money is too much, but you are good people."

Sophia sent another text to her assistant, giving her instructions to track down the driver's family, just in case something happened. She intended to keep her promise.

Frank swore. "What are you doing?"

She couldn't answer as the other car sideswiped them, attempting to knock them off the road.

"Gun!" Frank pushed her back to the floorboards. "Brakes," he yelled at the driver.

Glass from the window showered down on her and the cab's tires squealed against the pavement. The car rocked on its chassis at the sudden stop. She heard Frank scramble into the front seat.

"Move over!" Frank commanded the driver.

"What are you doing?" she asked, daring to sit up.

"He overshot us." Frank put the car in Drive and muscled the heavy car into a U-turn. He wasn't escaping, he was going on the offensive.

She was thrown back as Frank took control of the cab and floored it. Wind whistled through the broken window and she held her breath as he charged toward the attacking car.

She knew this wouldn't be the end of it. If they made it to the airport, if they survived the next leg in this convoluted journey, Halloran would just keep coming. They had to force his hand and dismantle Hellfire completely.

She pitched discretion out the window and sent Aidan a request to put a plainclothes bodyguard on the cabbie and his family until further notice. Frank wouldn't be happy she'd directly involved the company, but she'd soothe his ruffled feathers later. If they survived.

The engine labored and she and the driver were tossed around like rag dolls as Frank plowed into the path of the attacking car. It was a dreadful game of chicken and she knew Frank wouldn't be the first to blink. Bullets skittered off the hood and windshield, but the attacking driver veered at the last second.

Anticipating the move, Frank pulled hard on the wheel, managing to clip the front fender and send the other car spinning away. Frank stomped on the brakes, executed a three-point turn in record time and accelerated into the attacking car again.

Startled, she screamed, expecting an air bag to erupt from the steering wheel, belatedly remembering the cab was too old for those safety advancements.

As Frank backed away from the wrecked car and sped down the road toward the airport, she stared at the wreckage behind them until they rounded a curve.

The adrenaline spike plagued her. Her body couldn't be sure if she should be relieved or furious. Although she was grateful Frank's quick thinking and actions had saved them all, he'd put himself at risk in the process. He could've been killed.

It was a stupid thing to focus on now that they were safe. But safe was only temporary. Halloran was trailing them too easily and the greedy bastard held every advantage. She wouldn't let him win, wouldn't let him rob her daughter of a father all over again.

A renewed sense of purpose washed over Sophia, dulling the anger. She would do whatever it took to defeat Hellfire and Halloran. Frankie needed her father, and Sophia was determined to make that reunion happen.

Chapter Eight

Frank's concern grew exponentially with every hour. Sophia wasn't talking to him and he couldn't get a read on what was going on in that brilliant head of hers. She'd been friendly with the cabdriver, even sending him on his way with some cash and a business card, but she continued to give Frank the cold shoulder. She hadn't let him take her hand, hadn't allowed him the briefest moment to hold her close and assure himself she was in one piece.

He'd pulled their belongings from the locker while she'd scrambled for transportation. The fastest way out of the area was a short drive to Columbus, Ohio, so they retrieved the rental car and hit the road. While he kept an eye out for any pursuit, Sophia took care of the details with a charter flight service that expedited air travel for Leo Solutions. Despite his reservations, she was proving her point time and again that they needed what her company could offer.

"I've got a plane scheduled to get us from Columbus to Arizona," she said, breathing a sigh of relief.

"By now Halloran has people moving to intercept us no matter what we do."

"So we brave it out and keep pressing. It's worked so far."

He wasn't willing to trust in that kind of luck anymore today. "You ordered protection for the cabbie and his family, didn't you?"

Her chin came up and he stifled a smile at her marvelous defiant streak. "I did. He took care of us and we'll take care of him."

"I'm not disagreeing."

She stared straight ahead. "You don't have to worry that Frankie knows anything. I'm keeping your secret. No one at the company has any idea what I'm really up to."

He studied her. "You mean it."

"Of course I do."

"You're inviting a Hellfire attack."

That got a rise out of her. "That's inevitable. You know as well as I do we need to draw them out and distract them."

"What's really bugging you?" he asked after a few more minutes of silence.

She said his name, then stopped short, her teeth sinking into her full lower lip.

He wanted to pull over and soothe that small bite with a kiss. The need to taste her, breathe her in, was overwhelming. He wanted to run away with her, so far and so fast not even Halloran could find them.

Running away wouldn't fix anything. He'd still be officially dead, his wife would still be miserable and Frankie would be at Halloran's mercy.

"Turn off your phone."

"I've told you they can't track it."

"Do it anyway," he pleaded.

She powered it off and dropped it into her purse. "Why?"

"I want your full attention." Now that he had it, he forced the words out. "I'm sorry I scared you."

She snorted. "At the prison? I wasn't scared."

He spared her a long glance. "I was," he admitted.

"Okay, in the moment, yes, I was scared." She folded her arms over her chest. "Now I'm just angry. With you," she added as if he might miss the point.

"Want to give me a little more than that?" They had an hour left, plus the flight to Arizona. Better to get back on an even footing before Halloran's men caught up with them again.

"You took an impossible risk. You have to stop *doing* that."

He didn't know how else to protect her. "But—"

"We were a team once." She covered her face with her hands and let out a weary groan. Her hands in her lap again, she continued, her words aimed at the roof of the car. "It's as if you've forgotten I can hold my own. You aren't working alone. When Halloran's in custody—and he will be soon, by God—if you don't want to be a team anymore, that's okay with me."

His heart stuttered in his chest. Life without her had been unbearable, and not solely as a result of the pressures of working undercover.

"Frank, you're a father," she continued. "Grown or not, your daughter needs you. Stop behaving as if you're expendable."

This time he didn't interrupt the silence as it grew and swelled and filled the car to bursting.

Tucson, 6:45 p.m.

IT WAS NEARLY sunset when they stopped for the night at a roadside motel south of Tucson. Though they'd been able to clean up, change clothes and rest up on the private plane, they were both exhausted. Offices everywhere were closed, putting any direct search for Farrell on hold until morning.

After parking the rented SUV by the stairs, he peered through the windshield at their room. "Maybe I should sit out here and keep watch." It was agony spending so much time with her and not being able to connect on that intimate, passionate level they'd shared for so many years.

"And let them divide and conquer?" She shook her head, her glossy hair brushing her shoulders. "No way."

They towed the luggage up the stairs and settled into what was becoming a vexing routine. She set to work with her laptop and he brooded over his notes, adding in the new discoveries, looking for any weak spot or leverage.

His gaze and thoughts were drawn to her as unerringly as moths to flame. When he'd proposed, they had been madly in love, and with each year together it surprised him how they could grow apart and together and find themselves deeper in love.

Until he'd single-handedly wrecked everything, trashing her trust and faith in him. Somehow he had to make it right. Eliminating Hellfire would only be half the battle. He needed to make things right with his family, as well.

He had opened his mouth to unload everything building up inside him when she stood, her hands wrapped around her middle. "Are you okay?" he asked.

She closed the laptop, drumming her fingers on the lid. "I need a coffee or a soda or something."

He checked the change in his pockets. "I'll get it." Any excuse for a break from the cramped room and the feminine scent he remembered too well.

SOPHIA WATCHED HIM GO, fighting the sense that she was being unreasonable with him. Frank had buried himself in this mess for the right reasons. He wasn't her real enemy. No, that was Halloran and Farrell and Lowry and Engle and the rest of the convoluted Hellfire network. It frustrated her how connected Halloran was, how close they were at every turn. Thinking of the cab and the airport and everything else just kept adding up to one conclusion. Frank would obviously step in front of any stray bullet—or the equivalent—to save her.

While it was honorable and part of his nature, she couldn't abide any result that kept him from reuniting with Frankie. He seemed determined to prevent her from protecting him. They'd never worked that way. From the first moment they met, she'd appreciated the way he accepted her strengths and empowered her. She scolded herself again, rubbing another chill from her arms.

He'd let her talk with Eddie alone. He'd fought off one of Halloran's spies without her. They were finally making progress together. Being frustrated with the circumstances was no reason to make their task of dismantling Hellfire more difficult through a lack of communication.

It was past time to extend an olive branch. She'd always treasured the way they talked through everything. It hadn't escaped her notice that Frank avoided any mention of a future. Not that she could blame him. He'd been through so much with the nightmare of being abandoned by CID and the demands of chasing down Halloran.

She thought of the terrace on this level overlooking the pool. They'd passed it on the way to their room. It might be nice to enjoy the night air as they'd often done when Frankie was younger and chat about something other than their problems.

Grabbing a room key and slipping into her

flats, she headed for the vending machines, expecting to bump into Frank returning to the room. Immediately she knew something was wrong. Everything was too quiet. She glanced over the rail, breathing a sigh of relief that the rental car was still parked in the designated space below. At least he hadn't left her.

Though the dry evening air was cool against her skin, the chill she felt had nothing to do with weather. The vending machines were on the other side of the building, and even in this aging establishment it couldn't possibly have taken so long for him to find one stocked with a soda.

Just ahead, the bright light from the vending area spilled out over the concrete walkway. A large, lumpy shadow blotted out the light for a moment, then it retreated. Sophia caught the squeak of a rubber-soled shoe, a thud and a low grunt. She froze in place, two doors down from the vending machines that connected the parking lot side with the pool and courtyard side of the motel. Holding her breath, she caught the unmistakable swish and snap of a switchblade knife.

"Thelma?" she called out at the top of her lungs. "Which room are we in?" With any luck, no one by that name would be in a nearby room. In the answering silence, she hurried around the corner and into the vending area and skidded to a stop.

"One word and he's done." A younger man with sandy-brown hair and cold eyes held a knife to Frank's throat.

Sophia clapped a hand over her mouth, stifling the scream and the pleas that wanted to pour forth. She could hardly believe her eyes. Not only had they been found, but Halloran's oldest son had overpowered her husband with a knife. She shot Frank a bewildered look.

He gave her a look that urged her to play it cool.

"You're coming with me," the young man said. "Both of you."

Frank's gaze told a different story. He was playing along until a better opportunity to escape arose.

No point wasting time. "Mike Halloran," she said in her best maternal command, planting her hands on her hips as she stared down the son of Hellfire's leader. "What do you think you're doing?"

"Mrs. Leone." He shuffled his feet much as he'd done as a lanky preteen caught in a silly prank. "Yeah. Sorry. It's not as bad as it looks. This is just business."

Was it her imagination or had he eased the

knife back? "What kind of business requires you to attack an old family friend?"

"Dad wants to talk, that's all. General Leone hasn't been cooperating."

"Whether or not that's true, your mother would be appalled by this behavior. How is she?"

"Great." Mike relaxed further, leaving more than an inch between that gleaming blade and the skin of Frank's throat. "She spends most of her time in Saint Croix now."

Hopefully oblivious of her husband's treachery. "That's nice. She always loved the coast." Sophia took another step forward. "You realize no one talks business or anything else with a knife at their throat. Put it down."

Mike seemed to be debating how to carry out his orders. "Will you come along quietly?"

Of course not. "Certainly," she said. "Where are you taking us?"

"Back to my place until Dad can get here. He just wants to clear up this misunderstanding."

She bit back the sarcastic retort, refusing to look directly at Frank again as she nodded at Halloran's son.

"It coulda been just the general," Mike said. "But now that you've seen me…"

"I understand." She smiled. "We'll both come along. Put the knife away."

When Mike retracted the knife, Frank landed an elbow strike to his midriff, knocking the air from his lungs. The knife clattered to the tile and skittered toward Sophia. She scooped it up and pushed it deep into the back pocket of her jeans.

"Call the police!" Frank barked the order as he pushed Mike facedown.

"My phone's in the room." She looked around for anything they could use to tie up the younger man. "What do you want to do?"

Mike squirmed and Frank dropped to one knee, putting all his weight between the younger man's shoulder blades. "I say let his dad deal with him."

"Is that wise?"

"No," Mike said on a creaky exhale. "No. Let me go and I won't say anything. I'll tell him I couldn't find you."

Frank looked at her. "Do you believe him?"

"Not a bit," she replied. What she could see of Mike's face twisted and she shouted a warning half a second too late.

Frank, tossed off balance, fell backward and Mike, showing an aptitude for thug work, came at her.

"Get out of here!" Frank said, diving for Mike's legs.

The younger man tripped, regaining his balance with an agility she envied. Being older, and female, she had different options and skills to call upon, not the least of which was experience.

After Frank's trial and Frankie's recovery, she'd been brushing up on her self-defense skills. As a bonus, the increased activity had put her in prime shape for Frankie's wedding day. Now she was all the more thankful Aidan had joined Leo Solutions. Her future son-in-law was proving to be an excellent coach, willing to create fitness programs for anyone at the company, no matter their level or job description.

She let Mike close in, feinting and spinning out of his reach. Blocking his attack, she put a higher value on patience than her opponent did. She systematically moved the fight closer to the railing and the stairwell, places where her smaller size gave her a better advantage.

Mike countered with fast moves meant to confuse and intimidate. She managed to avoid the worst of it, but an evasive move left her with her back open to an attack.

She saw Frank's eyes go wide, his face a mask of panic. He had no way to help her. With Frank calling her name, aiming threats at Mike, she dropped to her knees and the young man went hurtling over the railing into the night.

A splash sounded as he hit the pool. Voices rose, cries of alarm and calls for help.

She peeked over the side, hoping to see Mike swimming to the edge, only to have Frank drag her back. "Phone cameras," he explained. "We have to go."

They ran for the motel room and gathered their belongings, making the rental car before anyone detained them.

"I can't believe Halloran had his son come after us," Sophia said as Frank searched for a safer place to spend the night.

"I'm not surprised," Frank said. "He was banking on the idea that I wouldn't hurt a kid the same age as my daughter."

"Unbelievable." Sophia stared out at the glowing lights as Frank merged with traffic on the interstate, aiming north. "I guess we're pushing the right buttons."

"I guess you are."

She reached out a hand to stop him. "*We* are."

"Right." His smile didn't reach his eyes. With little traffic, Frank reached the airport in less than half an hour. Per his habit, he drove a circuit of the airport hotels before choosing one and parking under the awning.

When they were settled into the new room,

she tried again to make him understand he wasn't alone. In this or anything else. "We're in this together, Frank."

"Much as I wish we weren't," he muttered. "The kid nearly hurt you."

"And he didn't you? He had a knife at your throat!" She reined in her temper. "I knew what I was doing."

"Sophia…" He sighed. "I'm trying to keep you out of danger."

"But that isn't realistic. Either we take risks and gather enough material for CID to work with or we get creative and take even bigger risks."

He slumped into a chair and raked his hair off his face. "Agreed."

She walked over and started rubbing at the knots in his shoulders. Although it wasn't the quiet fresh-air conversation she'd intended, it was still reminiscent of other pleasant moments they'd shared. "When Halloran and Hellfire are done, we should go home and get on with our lives." Frank's muscles tensed under her hands and she plowed on. "We had one cake tasting already. And Frankie plans to use Aunt Josie's recipe for a groom's cake."

Frank muttered something she took as approval.

She smiled to herself. "We'll need to choose

a caterer soon. I think Frankie wants me to go along for those appointments, to cast a deciding vote in case of any ties regarding the menu." She kept working out the kinks in his shoulders and chattering about Frankie and Aidan, willing Frank to want to be a part of their future as a family.

"Sophie, hush."

"It's adrenaline," she said in a lame attempt to defend herself.

"It is," he agreed. "Because I made a mess of things. I should've found a way to do this without you."

"You couldn't have."

"I know."

The regret in his voice tore at her. "Tell me something." She spoke to the top of his head, grateful he couldn't see the tears welling in her eyes. "Will you stay?" Her voice cracked on the query. Annoyed with the needs tangling in her chest, she tried again. "Will you stick around for Frankie? She'll believe me if I tell her you survived, but she'd rather hear she was right all along directly from you."

Frank came out of the chair and caught her hands, bringing them to his lips for a brief kiss. *"Dolcezza."* He kissed her hands again. "I promise to do what's best for all of you. I can't promise that will be staying around."

She opened her mouth to argue. To *insist* he come back into their lives. Knowing her too well, he tugged her close, silencing her with a claiming, searing kiss. She couldn't muster any energy to resist. All these months without him, to have him back, she just wanted to wallow in the scent, taste and touch of him. Her hands came up to frame his face and the kiss, rife with need and desire, sizzled through her bloodstream, only more powerful for the memories and familiarity of their long past.

She sighed, her breasts heavy and aching as she melted against his hard, muscled chest. Deep inside, she wanted to pretend this was just one more "normal" homecoming. Preferably the way the last homecoming should've been.

Her hands yanked at his shirt, eagerly seeking his warm skin. She trailed her fingers over the terrain she knew so well.

Holding her close, he turned her and lowered her to the bed, his body covering hers, gently pinning her to the soft mattress. Delicious. Her mind blanked out their troubles when he set his lips to her throat. His thigh wedged between hers, and his erection dug into her hip. She rocked her pelvis, needing him.

The sense of belonging overpowered her. Frank was her everything, always had been.

Except he wasn't promising her a future anymore. If Halloran had his way, there wouldn't be any future for the Leone family.

She savored one more kiss, sipping from his lips as tears stung her eyes. She couldn't do this, couldn't leave herself open to a repeat of the crushing loss she'd suffered when she thought he'd died. One last time, her body pleaded, but one last time would leave her devastated.

"Stop," she whispered against his lips. "Stop," she repeated when he raised his head to look into her eyes. She blinked quickly, unable to keep a tear from spilling over her lashes.

Frank brushed that tear away. "Are you sure?"

Her lips caught between her teeth, she bobbed her chin. At last she found her voice. "I can't do this." She felt awful, though she hadn't meant to lead him on. As much as her body wanted him, her heart *needed* him.

She simply couldn't invite that much pain into her life again. Not without some assurance that he wanted to rediscover and reclaim the relationship they'd lost.

Chapter Nine

Thursday, April 21, 7:05 a.m.

She'd rejected him. No amount of reviewing the facts changed that. On the motel room floor, Frank had tossed and turned all night wondering where he'd gone wrong.

Sophia had leaped from that bed as though it were on fire, when he'd been burning up inside to be with her. After fighting off Halloran's boy, Frank had needed to hold her, to assure himself she was okay—they were okay. He wanted to see and feel for certain the kid hadn't managed to hurt her.

She'd apparently needed and wanted something else. How had he misread the situation so completely?

He hadn't actually misread her, he decided as he reviewed last night once more. She'd been right there with him from that kiss up to the point he'd jerked his shirt over his head and fallen on her like a man starved for affection. Which he was.

After faking the suicide, he'd hidden for a while, courtesy of Torres. When the smoke had cleared, he'd poked at the fringes of Hellfire, piecing details together as best he could. He'd stayed far away from the temptation of Sophia in Seattle and Frankie in Savannah. Knowing he was to blame for his wife and daughter drifting apart motivated him to dismantle Hellfire sooner rather than later. Being aggressive had already gotten Torres killed. He couldn't allow his impatience to kill Sophia or Frankie.

The hardest months of his life had been pretending he didn't exist. Harder than infantry school in the summer. Tougher than winter training exercises in Korea. Too much solitude was bad for the soul, he'd decided early on. Yet the only person with whom he could maintain contact was dead now. Because of Frank's mistakes.

He prepped a second cup of the bitter in-room coffee, needing the caffeine jolt after another sleepless night. He'd been running on fumes since Torres's murder. What he wouldn't give for a restful night with his wife in his arms, her body soft and pliant, his every breath scented with the fragrance of her hair.

She'd always welcomed him home with a kiss, refreshing his soul. Just the way she'd done last night. Why had she pulled away from the connection both of them clearly wanted?

Had it been the visit with Paul Sterling? He hadn't said anything, but he could hardly begrudge her for moving on. She'd thought he was dead. He knew the moment the treason charge had been aimed at him that she would have to distance herself or go down with him.

His biggest regret was the timing. He'd been incarcerated when their daughter needed him most. Hearing about her injuries secondhand had been awful. He'd almost told Torres to go to hell with the undercover plan, that he'd take his chances and expose Hellfire before the evidence had been gathered.

A lot of good that had done. Frankie had healed, but he was still far from restoring his life or ensuring the ongoing safety of his family.

Halloran would definitely up the ante. It was only a matter of when and how. A man who would use his own son was capable of anything. Frank debated the wisdom of walking into the nearest federal authority and laying out the whole story. Except they believed he was the bad guy and he didn't have anything conclusive to prove otherwise. Yet.

He knew Sophia was sending tidbits of information to the reporter, to Eddie and probably to Leo Solutions as well, dribbling out details that would keep Halloran on edge. They needed to think bigger.

He glanced to the closed bathroom door blocking his view of his wife. She'd been eager to dangle herself like bait when they were in Alexandria. He could see that it might take something that tempting to draw Halloran into the open. Would Frank have the courage to let her do it if and when they needed that kind of ploy?

When she emerged, a silk tank tucked into faded jeans that hugged her gorgeous legs, he scalded his tongue on a gulp of the bitter coffee. He ignored the sting, eager to get busy and stay that way until the case was over. Today they would see if they could find anything incriminating in or around Fort Huachuca, Farrell's last duty station. When she bent to retrieve her bag, his attention zeroed in on her backside. He was definitely glad they were getting out of this room. The sooner the better.

Once they were on the interstate, Sophia said, "I asked my assistant to pull anything on his banking records or credit card activity. Paul said Farrell didn't care about money, only power and respect. That's harder to track."

"I've never seen Farrell accept a delivery. If

he's been riding a desk in an office, I would've missed him easily."

"With today's technology, he can probably do desk work anywhere in the world," Sophia said. "But we'll figure it out."

There was a piece he was missing. Frank's mind wandered, lulled by the sound of the tires on the asphalt. His brain sifted through memories and wound them up with daydreams. Why the hell had he thrown it all away?

He remembered how Frankie had come down the stairs, all dressed up and ready for her kindergarten graduation ceremony. He and Sophia had been near bursting with pride. His daughter had leaped from the next to last riser into his arms and giggled as he spun her in a big circle.

"Frank." A familiar touch gave his shoulder a shake. "Frank?"

"Huh?" He blinked away the haze of the memory, focusing first on the road and then on the worried face of the woman who wouldn't have him anymore. Damn it all. "What is it?"

"Trouble." The single word was loaded with urgency.

Adrenaline shot through his blood, clearing the last of the cobwebs. He checked his mirrors and came up empty. "Where?"

"Here." She turned up the volume and held

her cell phone so he could hear the video report on her phone.

A breaking news story named Frank as the prime suspect in the murder of Army CID Special Agent J.D. Torres. "Ruthless," he said with grudging admiration. The report didn't hold anything back, including a reward for any information that led to his arrest. "They'll name you as an accomplice soon."

"Probably by the end of the day." She pushed her phone into her purse as if it were infected with a vile disease. "At least we know we've become more than an irritation." She swore quietly. "I wanted to drive through the post and get a feel for the area, but it's too risky now."

"What about the bank?"

"After that news report?" She shook her head. "I really don't want to take a chance that your face shows up on any security feed."

"We can't give up now," he said. He refused to hide while she handled this alone. "Whatever Halloran does, however we choose to respond, we can't leave any member of Hellfire free to keep up the operation."

"I'm not giving up," she muttered. "I'm thinking."

"Think out loud, please." No way he'd make another assumption about what either of them wanted.

"Paul said he used that bank for a reason."

"A wink and a nod for a friend of Farrell?"

"That's my thought," she said. "The man is always scheming. I found out last night it's a privately owned bank, under the shelter of a corporate name."

"You didn't say anything."

"You were sleeping," she countered.

Doubtful, though he must have slept a little if he hadn't heard her working. "Did he trap you into opening Leo Solutions with him?"

She wrinkled her nose. "No. Just as he leaned on the friendship with Farrell, I leaned on the friendship with him."

Frank reached over and took her hand. "You were thinking of Frankie. I do understand."

Her mouth tipped up at one corner in a wry smile. "I think I'm starting to." Her breath caught. "Oh, dear God. I have to get word to Frankie."

Frank's gut clenched. "You need to convince her to lie low and stay away from reporters or anyone else asking questions."

Sophia fished her phone. "That won't be easy." Her fingers flew across the keypad. When she finished, she turned to Frank once more. "I'm thinking Halloran has something big planned."

"Meaning?" he prodded.

"With your face plastered all over the media, he thinks you'll be out of his hair."

"It does slow us down." When she didn't respond, he kept on driving, sticking with the plan until one of them came up with an alternative.

She mumbled a colorful oath in Italian. "We can't risk doing *anything* public here," she said. "They know we're in the area. With Lowry snagged, the contacts, text history and World Crossing employee badge, it's an easy guess we're here looking for something to tie up Farrell. One security camera and we're caught. Why else release that story that you're wanted for murder?"

"Which leaves us with no options?" He couldn't believe it, knew her mind was already racing ahead. In the army he'd been known for his superb strategic skills, but few people understood Sophia was his match.

"Turning you in would surprise him and it would backfire. Halloran would have you killed—for real—at the first opportunity."

Frank suppressed the shudder that shot through him at her words. If he died, who would protect Sophia and Frankie from Halloran's vindictive streak?

"Turn around. We can't go anywhere near Fort Huachuca."

He scanned the road for a place to turn around. "Where to?"

"We need another cheap motel with internet access so I can test another lead."

"What lead?" he asked as he took the next exit, only to swing back and head north, toward Tucson.

"It's something Paul said. The bank, Farrell riding a desk, the import-export and the CID. I can almost make the connections line up."

He was glad one of them could. Maybe he was too tired, but he wasn't following her train of thought. For Sophie it would only be a matter of time before things turned crystal clear. That small confidence was all it took to bring hope flaring anew in his chest. Sophia had been among the brightest military analysts in the CIA. Before his career ended hers by default.

"I should've brought you in on this from the beginning," he confessed.

"You did what you had to do," she replied, retrieving her phone from the depths of her purse again. "Head straight through the city."

"I thought you wanted to avoid security cameras."

"I do," she said. "More important, I want to be where they don't expect us to be." She put a finger to her lips as she raised her phone to her ear.

Listening to her side of the phone call, it baffled him when she asked to speak with someone. He didn't recognize the name at all.

"He'll take the call," she said. "This is Sophia Leone, General Leone's *widow*."

Oh, hell. Frank goosed the accelerator, joining the faster flow of traffic on the interstate. That was her determined voice, and a determined Sophia was unstoppable.

He really should've brought her into this at the beginning. All the reasons he'd kept her out of it seemed weak now.

Hindsight is always twenty-twenty, he thought. He'd reminded his soldiers of that countless times through his career. It was important to look back only long enough to learn from successes and mistakes. Then it was time to move forward.

He slid her one more glance, hoping like hell he could convince Sophia to move forward with him through the rest of his days.

Chapter Ten

Sophia ignored the ridiculous canned music assaulting her ear while she waited for Bradley Roth, the reporter who'd broken the Torres murder suspect story, to pick up. She knew he'd take the call and, if he didn't, she knew who to call next.

Beside her, she sensed the shift in Frank. He was exhausted but amused. And more than a little relieved they weren't going near an army post anytime soon. If her hunch played out, they might get away with lying low for another day or two, giving Halloran enough rope to hang himself.

As Frank navigated the traffic, she watched, half of her braced for another ambush. Based on the article she'd seen, if they'd continued to the fort, they'd have been caught for sure.

The story had gone national, making it too late to give the news to Frankie gently. Thank

God, Aidan was with her. He would get her through this and keep her safe.

"Bradley Roth," the reporter said, picking up the call at last. "Who's this?"

"Sophia Leone," she said, keeping her tone all business. "I saw the report pinning the Torres murder on my dead husband."

"Yes, ma'am. Do you have anything to add?"

She gave the reporter points for audacity and courage. "I suppose a retraction is out of the question?"

"My source is solid, Mrs. Leone."

"Your source must be thrilled to have someone take him at face value," she replied. "He's wrong."

"My source," Roth began, deftly avoiding any gender confirmation, "is above reproach. Unlike your husband."

"I'm not sure how often you've dealt with widows, Mr. Roth. We can be sensitive."

"Then let's cut to the chase so we don't prolong your distress."

"General Leone—"

"Former General Leone," Roth corrected.

She sighed loudly for effect. "The treason charge was fabricated. My husband was neither traitor nor killer."

Frank's hands clenched the steering wheel. She wanted to reach out to him. If only that sweet contact wouldn't leech the steel out of her voice. She needed every drop of it right now.

"Without any corroboration or proof from you, I can only assume your sensitive nature has you ignoring the facts and public record of his trial, the verdict and the new evidence recently discovered in the Torres case," Roth said.

She wanted to laugh as he used her turn of phrase against her. "Mr. Roth, you're being used. My family doesn't appreciate your sensationalized account that my husband is somehow alive and committing crimes. You can be sure I'll take decisive action against you and your employer."

"It's a free country and a free press, Mrs. Leone."

"Thanks in part to my husband and the troops he led," she said pointedly.

"Your own statement seals his guilt regarding the treason charge." Roth's initial curiosity about her was giving way to impatience.

"Ah, thank you for confirming your source," she said smoothly. "I'll let my assistant know what to do with your request when you call for an interview in a few days."

"Beg pardon?"

"Yes." She let the smile show in her voice. "I believe you will."

"Wait!"

She hesitated, let him think she'd disconnected. "Yes?"

"If you're so sure about the inaccuracy of my report, give me something to track down."

"Why should I help you do your job?"

"I'll print a retraction," Roth offered. "My influence can help shift the media tide in the general's favor."

"That's quite a claim." Her gaze lingered on her husband's white-knuckled hands. The traffic wasn't bad enough to warrant the reaction, so she assumed he didn't care for the game she was playing. Too bad. She couldn't let Halloran's gambit go unanswered. With everyone looking for Frank Leone, disgraced general turned killer, they were nearing time for a full frontal assault, and she wanted to be sure they were ready offensively and defensively.

"Although I'm sure you don't carry the clearance to see my original statement, I can assure you I did not testify against my husband." She paused when her voice started to shake. "You need to take a closer look at your source and his connections. I can assure you retired General Halloran has been abusing his authority for many years. In fact, I intend to prove he's smuggling drugs and laundering money through a privately held bank south of Tucson."

"Can you back that up?" Roth asked in a reverent whisper.

"I can," she said. "If you refrain from spreading more lies about my husband, I'll keep you in the loop as the evidence comes to light."

Beside her Frank gave a low whistle. She prayed Roth didn't hear it. "Do we have a deal?"

"Absolutely."

"I'll be in touch." Sophia ended the call, her hands trembling.

"What was that?" Frank asked through gritted teeth.

"An effective counterpunch," she stated.

"Is that a new synonym for *stupid*?"

"You're welcome." She sent another quick text message to Frankie and then turned off her phone. "We need to get to a motel."

"So you can manufacture evidence for another reporter?"

She refused to dignify that with a response. "A motel," she repeated. "Something out-of-the-way, cash only."

"I know how it's done," he said, his voice grim. "I've been living off the radar for months."

She clamped her lips shut while she counted

to ten. Then fifty. Not enough. Tears stung her eyes and she blinked them away.

She'd cried many nights, confused and hurt, when he turned distant before the last official army move to Washington. She'd cried, appalled and frustrated, when the treason charges were announced. When the verdict came down, she'd barely had time to absorb the news before they'd called her to identify the body.

"J.D. Torres was in the lab coat, wasn't he?"

"What?" Frank didn't spare her a glance as Tucson whizzed by the windows.

"When I identified your body," she clarified. "That wasn't a doctor. It was Torres in the lab coat."

Frank's sigh was plenty of confirmation. "Yes."

She sank into the memories, reviewing those strange, fractured days when she'd been pulled in so many directions. "Frankie was injured the same day you were charged with treason."

"I remember. The treason charge took me by surprise. I knew going undercover opened up the potential for things to get ugly, but I had no idea of Halloran's true reach."

The words dripped like ice water down her back. She shivered as horrible theories zipped around in her head. Tucson was fading into the distance before she found her voice. "Do you think…" She couldn't finish the thought. She started over. "Do you think," she repeated, her voice stronger this time, "Halloran arranged the attack on Frankie's convoy?"

"No." The one-syllable response was razor sharp and full of conviction.

A relieved breath shuddered in and out of her lungs. Her heart rate, stuttering a moment ago, settled back into a steady rhythm.

When they were several miles north of Tucson, the sunbaked desert stretching out on both sides of the highway broken only by a march of power lines and occasional, scrubby trees, Frank pulled to the shoulder and slammed the car into Park.

"What are you doing?" They needed to keep moving if they had any chance of outmaneuvering Halloran before the new shipment arrived.

Frank tossed his sunglasses onto the dash and scrubbed at his face.

"What's wrong?"

He wouldn't look at her. Instead, he pushed open the door and got out. He stalked a few paces ahead, turned and came back toward the SUV again.

She sat there, watching him as the minutes ticked by, wondering what the hell was going through his mind. She reached over and turned the key, cutting the engine. Pocketing the key, she got out of the SUV and leaned against the passenger door.

"What are you doing?" she demanded when he was only a few paces away.

"Bringing you in was wrong. Selfish. I can't put you through any more of this godforsaken chaos."

Weren't they ever going to get past this? "What I do and don't do isn't up to you," she snapped. "You lost the right to have an opinion about my activities when you took the easy way out."

"Easy?" He ran his fist along the scruff shading his jaw. "You thought that escape was easy?"

She folded her arms, waiting for him to say something worth a reply. She caught his eyes following the neckline of her silk tank. Her nipples peaked, responding to his gaze as though he'd touched her. Despite her best intentions, she couldn't seem to keep her raging desire for him in check.

"Looking at the facts, it seems as if it was easier to fake your death than share the truth with your wife."

"Sophie." He reached for her.

She twisted away. "Don't you touch me." She

was so weak around him, despite her anger and resentment for the choices he'd made. Choices that spelled the end of their family. Last night proved how easy it would be to slide into the comfort of old habits. To love and share each other as they'd always done, shutting out the world's troubles. "Thirty years of life and marriage and teamwork, and you just tossed me out."

"You know that's not what happened. I was protecting you."

"How would I know that? It was bad before Hellfire, Frank." She poked a finger into his chest. Saw the truth in his eyes. "You know it. Our relationship was going south before we moved to Washington." She clenched her teeth, determined to see this through. This wasn't the place to rehash the past, recent or otherwise. "Get back in that car and let's finish this."

"After what you just did, it's suicide to go to Seattle."

She did a double take, then heard herself cackling at his choice of words. She sounded half-mad and didn't much care. Finishing this, sticking with him to the bitter end, might just cost her her sanity. "Then we'd be closer to making the scorecard even. I called that reporter for—"

"Hell, no," he interrupted, his blue eyes flashing. "You made that call for yourself."

She hadn't stooped to such nasty fight tactics for more than a decade. Her molars would crack any second now if she didn't find a better way to maintain her self-control. "I made that call for Frankie," she finished stubbornly.

She wanted to give a victory shout when his shoulders drooped in defeat. "That's right," she continued. "I called that reporter, strung him along so you had a better chance of living long enough to reconcile with your daughter."

He stared at her, his jaw slack.

Mad as hell at herself as much as at him, she held up the car keys and aimed toward the driver's door. "Get in and do this my way or find another way out of this mayhem you created."

"I won't let you do this."

She turned, the heel of her tennis shoe grinding into the sandy soil, and stared him down. "Try to stop me, Frank. Just try."

Apparently the man's wisdom triumphed over his pride as Frank hopped into the passenger seat. His seat belt clicked as she merged with traffic on the two-lane road. With the voice app on her phone, she searched and found a regional airport a few hours away with more than one motel nearby. Even if Halloran caught their scent again when she ordered another flight from the charter service Leo Solutions used, he'd be hard-pressed to find them in time to do anything about it tonight.

Which was fine with her. She had her own agenda for the evening, and it revolved around getting even with the bastard and his cronies. She'd keep her promise about staying within legal lines, but there were ways to get her point across. Ways even Halloran couldn't misunderstand.

FRANK DIDN'T SPEAK again until they were in a room on the first floor of a family-owned motel. What could he say? She was right about all of it, and, though he and Torres had made progress, without Sophia he wouldn't be able to topple Halloran's operation.

He pulled the curtains closed and took note of the few amenities while she booted up her computer. He wanted to apologize for everything he'd done wrong in recent years. There had to be something he could say to crack that wall of ice she was hiding behind now. She was his wife, damn it. At one time he'd known her better than he'd known himself. In light of his recent choices, he still knew her better. On the other hand, he hardly recognized the man he saw in the mirror anymore.

"You and Frankie were always the most important pieces of my life."

She lifted her gaze, taking his measure over the rim of her reading glasses, her brown eyes clear and emotionless. "I know."

"Everything I did, every choice good or bad…" He didn't bother finishing when her attention returned to her laptop. "Sophia," he said, not above begging at this point. He desperately needed to clear the air.

"I'm listening."

She wasn't—her eyes were skimming through whatever she'd found on the display. A rosy glow lit her cheeks, and her lips parted with excitement. "Good Lord."

"What now?"

"Farrell and Paul." She glanced up at him again, her eyes lit with excitement. "I've been thinking about his quip about clients and the cybersecurity program."

"He pretty much confirmed Farrell is part of the import-export team."

"Right." She pursed her lips for a second. "He said Farrell once worked at World Bridge Shipping."

"I assumed he just mixed up the name."

"He did." She leaned back in the chair, pointing at the screen. "Look."

Frank squinted, didn't see what had her so excited. "Help me out. What am I looking for?"

"It's been right under my nose, to quote Paul again," she muttered. "He had a private client list and kept World Crossing, Incorporated, listed under a different name. The phone numbers and website addresses match."

"Holy crap." He stood. "This is good news, right?"

"This puts us in the driver's seat." She opened another window and started typing again. "Frank, how had you been tracking incoming shipments?"

"I followed a hunch. Halloran spent some time with a transportation unit early in his career. Torres had started digging through the shipping reports on military gear coming back to the States. Some of the weights didn't add up." As he spoke, she made notes, and he knew she was locked on to every word. "After the verdict, I started staking out East Coast ports according to a pattern Torres suspected. I never thought about the import-export broker, but I noticed the same freight line at every destination and went from there."

"Makes sense," she said.

"You remember the next shipment is due any day."

"And we can be sure Halloran is there to meet it," she announced.

The brilliant smile she aimed at him might as well have been a hot dagger through his heart. The idea of his enemy within his grasp was almost too much good news. "What do you mean?"

"I think I can access the World Crossing computers in Seattle."

"Remotely?" he asked, praying she'd say yes.

"No." She bit her lip. "Once we're on-site, it shouldn't be a problem. We can download files and give CID the info they need to move on Halloran and Hellfire."

"Besides the fact that it's illegal, it could get you killed trying. We don't know where Engle and Farrell are." He felt miserable watching how his response—his logical response—dulled the happiness on her face.

"If we can link Halloran to this company, if we can show abuse of the contract or find evidence of drugs on-site, CID can take it from there." She frowned at him. "You've wanted to intercept that shipment from the start."

"I want to force him to do something incriminating, yes," Frank hedged. He didn't want her there when things got ugly. He pulled up a chair. "Teach me what to do and I'll go in."

She shook her head. "I'll probably have to finesse things a bit." Her smile was back in an instant. "I've booked us a plane to Seattle early in the morning so we'll be ahead of the shipment. We can fine-tune how to get into the office at the port once we see what we're dealing with."

"I've been on shipping piers and docks, Sophie." He'd met their enemy firsthand and hated the danger he'd be escorting her into. "There are so many risk factors. Are you sure remote access isn't an option?"

She removed her glasses and pressed the heels of her hands to her eyes. "All right. Let me see if I can find another path."

He waited while her fingers moved swiftly and quietly over her keyboard. Whatever she was doing, she muttered and grumbled here and there as she poked at the system software. It was his last respite. When she was done with this attempt, he had to come clean about the rest of it. He had to unburden himself and give her a chance to forgive him, just in case the worst happened when they finally caught up with Halloran.

"Oh, good," she said without much enthusiasm. "My laptop is connected with the Leo Solutions network. I can fiddle with a few things." Her teeth nibbled on her lower lip as she continued. "We'll see if that causes a stir. I want to make them sweat."

"What next?"

"Not much until we're on-site." She closed her laptop and set it aside. "Then I suggest we kick ass."

He nodded, knowing what he had to do now. It could very well be his last night alone with her. "Sophia?" he began, dredging up the courage to continue.

"Yes?"

This would be so much easier if he'd never left her out of his professional decisions. Better to just spit it out and let her start hating him now. "You mentioned how things changed before our last move." The abrupt wariness in her eyes didn't make this easier. His heart pounded. "Things changed because that's when I first met Torres," he confessed. "CID wanted help with a soldier in my command who'd flipped out and joined the local resistance."

He could practically see the wheels turning behind her eyes as she rewound reports and news footage to that time.

"The Penderson case?" She sat back in the chair, pulling her knees up to her chest.

He wasn't surprised she'd figured it out immediately. While situations such as the Penderson case were rare, very few people had access to the full facts and circumstances. Sophia would've been one of a handful of analysts cleared for the details and, still, she didn't know the worst of it.

"Why you? What could you possibly have known about some morally conflicted private?"

He sank onto the edge of the bed. Her reaction to this could break him, but he couldn't be a coward any longer. "I didn't know the soldier as well as I knew the family he killed."

That warm brown gaze turned chilly. "Knew them how?"

He could see she was already willing to believe the worst—that he'd turned into one of those men with no self-control who took up with women to scratch an itch during deployments. "I was trying to grease the wheels to get one of their sons to the States. I called a few friends in DC looking for a favor."

"You didn't call me."

"No."

She took a deep breath, studying him. "What really happened, Frank? It's not unprecedented to help locals who go above and beyond while we're working in their country. Nothing like that was worth hiding."

And yet he had hidden things from her and

all his reasons seemed flawed as he tried to explain. "Penderson shot up a village. He went after that particular family because of me. I'd sought them out to thank them for their service and to grieve with them. The father and son lost their lives in an action that saved my men. It was a gruesome act. I'll never understand why Penderson murdered the rest of them."

"Oh, Frank." She moved to sit beside him on the bed, tucking her feet under her. She rubbed slow circles over his back. "Why didn't you tell me?"

For a moment, he reveled in the miracle of having her close. "The army needed me out there to keep things from falling apart while they investigated Penderson's motives and influences."

"You had the authority to be respected by both sides," she said with a comprehending nod.

"We found Penderson's body about ten days later." The butchered remains of the errant soldier had been laid out on the side of a hill, in full view of the main road into the base. The army cleaned it up swiftly, managing to smother all pictures, but Frank had been carrying that grisly image and the guilt ever since.

She took one of his hands in both of hers, smoothing the flesh over and over until his fist relaxed. "I remember. None of that was your fault."

"Maybe not directly. Penderson wasn't the only soldier on that base who'd become a sympathizer. Rooting them out was like kicking a nest of rattlesnakes."

"I didn't hear anything about that."

"The army prosecution focused on other charges. Sex trafficking in particular," he said pointedly. "Halloran's son was among those arrested."

"Mike? No way."

"Yes. He dodged the worst of it, thanks to his dad. Torres and I always suspected he was actually the ringleader."

"Things get very strange out there."

"They do," he agreed. Her touch soothed him as nothing had in years. He was ready to beg, borrow or steal more than the basic comfort she was offering. "Sophia, you have to know I wasn't one of those guys out there."

Her palm soft on his cheek, she turned his face toward hers, blessed him with a sweet kiss. "I know. I know you, Frank." Her lips were delicate as rose petals against his. "I trusted you implicitly."

"Until I shut you out."

"Even then I trusted you," she countered in a voice as gentle as her touch. "It hurt me when you pulled away, but I trusted you to come around."

"And I let you down." He shouldn't let her close, couldn't force himself to be honorable and pull away. "It wasn't supposed to go that way. The sex operation sting, connecting with the drug lord, Hellfire was supposed to welcome me with open arms, not pin me down with treason charges."

"It's okay," she crooned. "We'll get out of this. Together."

He scooted away from her warm body, and those few inches felt like miles. "Torres and I were sure Halloran would have me killed. Coming clean at that point would've given Hellfire room to escape with their money and no consequences. I wouldn't have left you if we'd thought there was a better option. I swear it. They'd already made one attempt during a transport to see if I'd flip on him."

"You passed."

"Of course." He leaned forward, elbows on his knees as he rubbed his temples. "It was weak and obvious, but it was enough to convince me Halloran had spies everywhere."

"Still does, apparently," Sophia agreed. "Is that everything?"

"Yes." He felt clean, almost weightless now that she knew. "I'm so sorry, *dolcezza*."

"You did what you had to do."

"You have my word," he promised, "I will never let you and Frankie down again and, if you will allow me in your lives, I will spend the rest of my life being there for you and proving in everything I do how very much you both mean to me."

"You are all I've ever wanted, my love."

The phrase caught his full attention. "You…" He was afraid to ask her to repeat the sentiment.

"I've never stopped loving you, despite how infuriating you've been recently."

"But—"

"Hush. Don't ruin the moment," she warned, pressing a finger to his lips. "Just accept it and count your blessings."

"You. You are my blessing."

"Promise to remember that from this day forward?"

"Yes." He stole a kiss from her smiling mouth. "Promise not to take it back?"

She laughed. "I promise."

He kissed her soundly, letting all his hope and passion and need pour out, pour into her. He felt whole at last as she accepted him, her heart pounding against his. The sun could rise tomorrow or fall into the ocean—he had the most important element in his world in his arms at last.

SOPHIA GAVE HERSELF up to the irresistible desire Frank's touch invariably ignited. His reticence and distance were at last well and truly gone. Under her hands her husband felt like himself again. There was tension, a by-product of their mutual excitement, but the secrets and guilt that had been lurking beneath the surface had disappeared.

Here was the man she'd loved with her whole heart and spirit. Her body trembled with the need to love him again.

"Frank," she whispered over and over, kissing every part of him within reach. The rough whiskers at his jaw, his ear, his corded neck. He mirrored her movements, teasing her and reacquainting himself with all the places that elicited her passionate reactions. That tender place behind her ear, the ticklish spot at the base of her throat.

One of his big hands cruised over her hip, holding her tight to him, while the other cupped her breast, teasing her nipple through the fabric of her tank and bra.

She'd known his body since they were young twentysomethings, before he'd filled out and she'd gone softer with motherhood. Fit and able, they'd been blessed with good health and a hefty dose of humor as they'd matured. She didn't want to be anywhere but here in this precious place they created, just the two of them.

Her hands worked the buttons of his shirt until the panels fell open and she could devour his muscled chest with her hands, eyes and mouth. Amid gasps of anticipation and breathless kisses, they rediscovered and reclaimed all that they'd missed.

Impatient, she tugged off her tank top and bra while he dealt with his boots. When he'd stripped away his pants and her jeans, they fell on the bed together, giddy as teenagers, eager and awkward and in a desperate hurry to make up for lost time.

He settled her with long, sensual strokes and touches, kisses across her collarbone and lower to her breasts. She breathed in his scent, rising to his tantalizing mouth as he suckled on one nipple and then the other. She sifted her fingers through his salt-and-pepper hair, the texture so familiar despite the longer length.

He feathered kisses over her quivering belly to the juncture at her thighs. As he parted her legs with his broad shoulders, she knew he was settling in for a long siege. At the first flick of his tongue on her sensitive flesh, she bucked and tried to squirm away. His heavy hand held her in place and she had to plead with him.

"I need you inside." She wanted that intimate unity above anything else. "Please, Frank. Now."

It didn't take much coaxing. Rising over her, he nudged at her entrance. She was so ready for him. He plunged deep, hard and hot inside her. Joined completely with him, she knew he felt that priceless sense of connection as keenly as she did. Tears of joy blurred her vision and she smiled up at him, savoring the homecoming they'd been denied for so long.

"I missed you, *dolcezza*." Braced over her, he rolled his hips, stroking her body inside and out.

He felt amazing in her arms. The laughter bubbled out of her in simple, pure delight of being together, body and soul. Her whole body clutched around him as she ran her hands over every part of him. His powerful arms and shoulders, his wide back, down to his hips.

He knew precisely how to move to heighten and extend their pleasure. It seemed a lifetime of practice hadn't been lost or forgotten while they were apart. She knew him, too. She kissed his throat, raked her nails gently down his sides while her legs cradled his hips.

When at last he drove her up and over that sensual peak, the climax hit her full force, leaving her gasping for air as stars flashed behind her eyelids. He found his release a moment later, his body shuddering before he collapsed over her in sheer bliss.

A minute or an hour might have passed in that beautiful, euphoric state until at last he rolled away, pulling her back tight to his chest. He snuggled her close and wrapped her in his arms. She'd fallen asleep this way almost every night they'd been together during the course of their marriage. When his breathing eased, becoming the rusty snore she'd missed so desperately, she let the tears fall once more.

They weren't done or safe, but she felt confident that together they could conquer any new obstacle Halloran or anyone else placed in their path.

Chapter Eleven

Frank woke before the sun, content and refreshed, with Sophia's warm, generous curves tucked beside him. It had been over a year since he'd slept so well and she'd been beside him then, too. He pressed a kiss to her silky sable hair, determined to make this the first day of the rest of their lives together.

He was indulging in a daydream of life after Hellfire when her cell phone hummed with an incoming message. It shouldn't have been enough of a sound to wake her, but her eyes popped open. Her gaze tangled with his and her smile bloomed.

"Good morning." He kissed her softly, before she could roll away and be distracted by their problems. "I'll shower while you check on that."

"Okay." She seemed almost shy today. "It's the pilot. The plane is ready when we are."

He grinned and kissed her again. His body was primed for the upcoming confrontation and he finally felt as though he had his head on straight. They'd get to Seattle and put an end to Halloran's operation once and for all.

A few minutes later, with a towel wrapped around his hips, he opened the door to let the steam from his shower dissipate and caught her pacing. She wore only his blue button-down shirt from yesterday and he took a moment to admire the excellent view of her shapely legs.

Then she turned and he saw trouble stamped on her face. "What happened?"

"There was a cyber attack on Leo Solutions last night," she said, brushing by him to take her turn in the bathroom. "You can read the email while I shower. I'll be ready in ten minutes."

He dressed quickly, lacing up his boots by touch as he read the email outlining the situation. According to his future son-in-law, someone had tried to hack into the cloud servers, using administrative codes previously assigned to Paul Sterling.

Frank wanted to punch something. "I need a target," he muttered. Hearing the water shut off in the bathroom, he read the entire report once more.

Aidan relayed assurances that no data had

been lost and all client information and systems were in order. He said the closest thing to a breach had been in the financials. The attacker had been focused on battering down the firewalls with no success.

Naturally, Frank thought. This had Hellfire and Farrell written all over it. On a whim, he checked his offshore account and found the balance had doubled overnight. Hellfire planned to pin everything about the drug operation on him.

"Did you read it?" Sophia asked as she came into the room, toweling her wet hair.

"Yeah. Not the ideal way to meet my future son-in-law."

Her eyes widened, and then her smile seemed to set her whole face aglow. "At least you know he's competent." Sophia explained a few of the more technical details of the attack while she dressed, and they were out the door within ten minutes, as promised.

On the way to the airport, he told her about the money and his theory that they were framing him up tight.

"We won't let them," she said. "I'll have a team make sure nothing managed to get added to our servers or accounts that would put us or our clients in a compromising position."

He thought it through, reading the email on

her phone one more time while the private pilot waited for clearance to take off.

"Sterling claimed Farrell didn't care about money," he said once they were in the air.

"Right." Sophia arched an eyebrow, then both eyebrows, as his meaning dawned on her. "Power and respect are his priorities. The money is disposable." She tapped her fingernails against the arm of the seat. "I am sure he's using that bank somehow. I just need to find a transaction."

He knew what she was trying not to ask. "Go ahead and have your team pick apart the offshore account." From what he knew about his daughter, that wasn't her area of expertise. Hopefully, giving in on this would be a compromise to the request he knew she'd make as soon as they landed.

He let her work while he considered the best way to breach the import-export brokerage offices.

When the pilot started the descent, Frank felt the pressure dragging at him again. It was all he could do to stand tall and hide the stress beating at him as they collected their bags and picked up a rental car, another Leo Solutions company perk.

"Well, they'll know we arrived," he said, following the signs toward the waterfront.

"I don't want it to be a secret," she said. "After last night, I'm done hiding."

"Have you found any record of Halloran or Farrell in the area?"

"Not yet. I have feelers out. You know she'd love to see you," she suggested quietly.

Naturally, she'd seen straight through him to the root of the problem. He never should've opened up last night. The relief of her forgiveness only intensified his desperate need to be sure she remained safe.

"Ask anything else," he said, ignoring the desperation in his voice. "I can't see her until I know this is over."

"You walked into a prison for me," she said, trying to lighten his mood. "This is your daughter."

"It's different." The guilt and shame were like grains of sand chafing at his skin. "Let's finish this first."

Despite how he and Sophia had reconnected last night, he wouldn't presume he could stay in her life or Frankie's in the same capacity as before. Forgiveness was more than he'd expected. If only they allowed him to be a small part of their lives, it would be enough. It would take time for them to trust him after all the lies and deceptions.

"All right," Sophia said, reaching across the

console to rub his shoulder through his jacket. "Halloran probably has someone keeping tabs on her anyway."

He hated that it was true. "He'll expect you to ditch me in favor of protecting her."

"She's capable of protecting herself and the company," Sophia said. "And she has her own kind of backup."

"You like him a lot, don't you?"

"More than that. I adore Aidan. You'll see when you meet him and see them together. Victoria recruited him away from Interpol."

"She has an eye for investigative talent," he said, keeping to the safer portion of this topic.

"Yes, she does. We're very fortunate as a company and as a family to have friends like Victoria and Lucas."

He did his best not to get his hopes up at the way she automatically included him in their future. From the moment he'd had to start lying to her, his secret hope had been that one day they could manage a genuine reconciliation. Now he wasn't sure he could get them all through this nightmare alive.

Halloran had had years to perfect his team, to increase his reach and influence. What chance did he and Sophia really have at stopping him at this late hour? "You're sure the data at Leo Solutions is secure?"

"Yes. With every update from the team, we're all more convinced it was primarily a distraction."

"So we wouldn't notice what?"

"That's the big question," she said. "The computers and servers have been scrubbed for viruses, malware and data tampering. We can even show our customers how secure everything is if this gets out."

"It won't." He wouldn't let it. One way or another, Halloran's threat to his family ended here.

Down near the waterfront, he chose a decent independent hotel with a vacancy sign. "Will this work?"

Sophia grinned. "Like a charm. Ready to make some heads roll?"

Her expression was contagious. When had he allowed himself to forget her inherent fighting spirit? Probably while he was in exile berating himself for not trusting her with the truth from the beginning.

They checked in, a valet whisked away the car and a bellman carried their bags up to the room. "It's better service than our honeymoon," she murmured when they were in the elevator.

The memories put another kind of contagious smile on her face. He wanted to talk about what came after, but he was afraid of getting ahead of himself.

She seemed to understand, declaring the signal was fantastic when they reached the hotel room of the day and her computer was up and running.

"One more positive sign," he said, shrugging out of his jacket. "How can I help?"

"First, we have to confirm Halloran and Farrell are here." She pointed him to the phone in the room. "I'll let you do the honors."

He entered the numbers she gave him and listened to the phone ring several times. He was about to give up when a rough voice answered, "World Crossing."

"This is Halloran. I need a status report," Frank demanded.

"No sign of trespassers. Container is offloaded and heading this way now."

"Good." Frank replaced the receiver and grinned at Sophia. "Worked like a charm. The guy who answered said the container is there and trespassers are not." The hired help had no reason to question the identity of anyone who had the right number to call.

"Then let's go." She pulled her hair back into a ponytail. "This is the perfect time for me to try to break into their computer."

"You promised to try it remotely," he said.

"And I failed." Tucking her phone and a flash drive into her pocket, she started for the door.

He knew it was a losing argument and they were wasting time. "On one condition."

She paused, sending him an expectant look over her shoulder. "Which is?"

"I'm in charge." He stowed a camera, binoculars and his notebook in his various pockets. Then he added his gun and handed her the knife they'd taken from Halloran's son.

"All right, General." She stepped aside. "Lead the way."

He didn't expect the cooperation to last, but it gave his heart a moment to catch up with the idea of leading her into danger.

SOPHIA WAS CERTAIN she could draw Halloran out with the right incentive and she was certain that incentive was on the World Crossing computers. Money wouldn't be enough. By now he and the rest of his crew had their wealth hidden away and protected.

It helped that Eddie was archiving her reports and her new reporter pal Bradley Roth had already run a follow-up based on the few pieces of Frank's puzzle she'd felt safe sending him. Still, after the cyber attack and the windfall deposit into Frank's offshore account, she knew nothing short of a confession would pull the noose tight around Halloran's neck.

"Got him," she said as Frank approached the pier that was home to the shady import-export brokerage.

"Say again?"

She laughed at Frank's slide into a more military lingo. "I just got confirmation Halloran is in Seattle." She showed him a grainy surveillance picture from a camera at the airport. "He arrived last night."

"You can't honestly believe he'll personally oversee the arrival of a drug shipment. He considers himself the deal maker, not the labor."

"He didn't come to Seattle just for the golf."

"It is a tourist destination, Sophie."

She loved it when he sweetened her name that way. Only him. "Then score another point for us. We're not here for tourism—we're focused on bringing Kelly Halloran to justice."

"Retired General Drug Lord." Frank swore. "It still pisses me off."

For just a moment, she let herself envision immediate success and what might come next. With Frankie and Aidan capable of running Leo Solutions, would Frank want to modify their original plans and travel more? One minute she thought she knew the answer; the next a flood of different questions rolled through her mind. The only thing she knew beyond any doubt was how much it would break her heart if he got hurt or couldn't see them as a couple the way they used to be.

"We'll walk from here." Frank parked in a space close to the main street and came around to open her door. "We'll stick together." He tipped her chin his way, holding her gaze. "I mean it. If I say we're done, I don't want any argument."

She gave him her most cooperative smile along with the verbal reassurance. He rolled his eyes, knowing her far too well. In the past she might've added a salute, but today the gesture would be more exasperating than humorous. It was becoming clear that however they cleared his name, his career was over. She wondered if he was already lamenting the loss of that lifestyle or if he was struggling with what to do with retirement now that the business they'd planned was up and running and in capable hands.

They walked together down the docks as if they were looking for one of the several import-export businesses scattered among the warehouses. This was a working terminal rather than one converted to retail, and the scents of fuel, oil and heavy machinery mingled with the cleaner aromas on the sea air. It was a strange combination that put Sophia in mind of healthy industry and thriving business. It angered her that Hellfire tainted that with their illegal activities.

"There's the office," she said, pausing to peer into the window.

"Easy, tiger."

In the past, she would've bristled at the admonition. Now she just stifled a smile, knowing he was right. Impatience here could get one or both of them killed. "There are times when your cool-and-collected routine drives me up a wall," she teased.

"More fun for me," he said.

She glanced up at his face and caught the smirk. "Think Hellfire will agree with our definition of fun?"

The smirk turned edgy. "Absolutely not." He lifted his chin a fraction. "We've got company."

"Took longer than I thought it would."

"They can afford to hang back now," Frank said. "They know if we had the evidence it would be over already. The only way to get stronger evidence is to get closer."

"They *think* they know," she corrected. The piece about the adjusted weights on official contracted shipments might be Hellfire's downfall. "Why don't we just go right in?"

"Because they would capture you as soon as you crossed the threshold." He shoved his hands into the pockets of his jacket. "Not a chance I'm willing to take."

He had to know taking chances would be required to wrap this up quickly. Like him, she couldn't imagine losing him to that kind of aggressive maneuver. Not without the right backup. Backup Frankie and Aidan could provide if Frank would stop being stubborn.

They were nearing the end of the pier, coming as close as visitors were allowed to the unloading area. Cranes slid and scraped back and forth, groaning with the load of some containers. Diesel engines rumbled, the sound broken only by the call of gulls wheeling in the sky.

"He can't possibly have a full container of drugs," she muttered, unable to imagine a bust that big.

"Drugs, money, military equipment. It's likely combined."

Knowing he was right didn't make it easier to stomach. If she blurted out all the violent thoughts in her head, expressed every dire, vengeful idea, he'd never let her help. She recognized the recklessness and reined it in, unwilling to let her emotions jeopardize the ultimate goal of restoring her family.

When Frank turned to walk back up the pier,

she followed, her mind turning over more options. Halloran had put all the right pieces in place, recruiting the people with the power to make things run smoothly. How could they dismantle that definitively? There were chinks such as Lowry in the armor, but Halloran would replace those people, shore up the weaknesses and keep right on banking the profits. Frank couldn't have his life back and none of them could rest until they cut the head off this long-tailed snake.

"What are you thinking?"

"Pretty much the same thing I've been thinking," she replied. "Aside from racking my brain for a contact within the port authority, I'm trying to decide how we can get Halloran into the open where some decent, honest person with the right sort of badge can arrest him. If he slips away, he'll start over. Even if your name is cleared in the process, someone else will be vilified. Much as I hate to admit it, the cyber attack and the money transfer worry me."

"I know."

The grim, resigned tone caught her attention. "What are *you* thinking?" It better not be another self-sacrificing idea.

"I want a bird's-eye view," he said, nodding toward the high-rise buildings on the other side of the access roadways running between the dock and the city.

They left the car parked and walked away from the pier, knowing Hellfire spies watched every step. It was all she could do to ignore them. She wanted to taunt them, to dare them to make a move. Again, too reckless. She was better than those self-destructive urges.

"He destroyed our family," she said when they found a place that gave Frank an effective overview of the pier. "I want him to pay for that."

"Does Eddie handle civil suits now?"

"Stop." She bumped his shoulder with hers. "You know what I mean."

"Uh-huh," he said, preoccupied with whatever he saw through the binoculars.

He had always known what her heart needed—frequently before she did. That intuition of his was probably why they were out here in broad daylight when he'd rather be safely ensconced in another motel room.

While Frank studied the pier, Sophia's gaze shifted north, toward her house on Queen Anne. She hadn't been gone a full week, but she missed it. Temptation rode her at every turn. Her house, a home she'd never shared with Frank, felt as if it were within walking distance. She wanted to dump the suitcase and sleep in her own bed beside her sexy husband.

But it was her husband, larger than life, that presented her biggest temptation. Her palms itched to touch him, to reassure her body and heart that he wouldn't disappear again. Would anything ever convince her?

Now that they'd been blessed with a second chance, she wanted him back in her life like before. Forever. She needed to reclaim the dreams they'd shared, and unless she was wishfully misreading his signals, he wanted that, too. The sooner they had Halloran trapped, the better. There was a wedding to plan.

"I need some air," she said suddenly. "Didn't we pass a vending machine?"

His eyes met hers and her feet froze in place. "You aren't going alone."

"I am." Making love had turned her overprotective husband into a nearly obsessive guardian. She rolled her shoulders back. "I thought I'd go for a walk."

His laughter cracked like a whip through the small room. "Not alone. You're not going out there as bait, Sophie."

"We have to do something. What do you suggest?"

"Carpet bombing comes to mind," he said. "Take a look." He handed her the binoculars.

She adjusted the view in time to see a fork-lift heading up the pier to Hellfire's warehouse. It carried a sand-colored container labeled with an army code. "No way." She dropped the binoculars to stare at Frank. "You think this is another tweaked contract shipment?"

"Yeah." The camera whirred as he took burst shots. "That number is for armored vehicle parts."

"Parts that must be padded with contraband." She watched a bit longer, awestruck by the audacity. "We need to get our hands on the computer records." Lowering the binoculars, she turned to her husband. "They're so damned sure of what we will and won't dare do. Why don't we throw them a curveball?"

Anything to go on the offensive. It wasn't in her nature to sit back indefinitely, hoping the right things would happen. "We have a family to reunite and wedding plans to adjust accordingly," she reminded him.

He looked away. She told herself it wasn't personal, that he was focused on fixing the bigger threat of Halloran—and rightly so—before he could focus on renewing their personal life.

And hadn't she told him those decisions could wait? She'd told herself she wouldn't pressure him into doing what *she* wanted. He'd been exiled from everything he'd known and loved. That experience had to have an effect. She needed to give him the time and space to adjust.

Except she didn't see anything so different from the man she'd fallen for, married and built a life with. He was the same in all the ways that mattered. Focused, strong, determined. Protective and honorable. His choices, though difficult on all of them, proved it. Why couldn't he see himself through her eyes?

"Hang on." His jaw clenched, the muscle in his profile jumping.

"Frank?"

"We're staying put," he said in that ironclad tone no argument would overcome. "Farrell is here." He dropped the binoculars and raised the camera once more.

A ripple of excitement coursed through her body. She wanted to get down there immediately. "Mr. Accounts Receivable. Can we intercept him?"

"And what would we do with him?"

She arched an eyebrow, her silence speaking volumes.

"Aside from tear him limb from limb," Frank said. "Or demand statements that won't hold up in court."

She jerked her thumb toward the pier. "He's diverting at least one container labeled for military use," she said. "That will get someone high on the food chain involved, right?"

"If the someone offering up the tip isn't wanted for treason, fraud and now murder."

She swore against his logic. "Mitigating circumstances. I'm calling the police unless you have a better suggestion."

He sighed as he put his camera back in his pocket. "I'll create a distraction and you do what you can."

"Just you and me?" Did he think she wouldn't notice his avoidance of Leo Solutions' resources?

"I'll need a two-minute head start," he said as they crossed the street once more. "When all hell breaks loose, you can go in and do what you can."

She caught his shirtfront before he could dash off and planted a kiss on his lips. It was quick, but it sizzled right through her. "Be careful."

He nodded, a smile slowly spreading across his face. "You, too. We'll meet back here."

During her two-minute delay, Sophia sent a text to Frankie: Don't worry, sweetie. We're all going to be okay. Her time up, she strolled down the pier, walking with purpose but not fast enough to draw attention. It didn't really matter. Halloran's men knew who she was, and though she couldn't see them, she knew they had to be watching.

FRANK STUCK TO the shadows of equipment waiting to be put back in use, clearing every corner and roofline. The spies were gone or had found better perches. No one was watching the pier at all right now. Frank counted his blessings and pressed on.

Getting in and out would be easier at night, but if they waited, any product or evidence might be gone. As he searched for the right distraction, he thought an explosion would be ideal. He'd love to plant it in the heart of World Crossing and call the mission complete. Except that left Halloran out there free to start over with a different crew.

One thing he'd learned since going undercover for CID was how many people could be manipulated for the smallest stakes. It made him wonder what kind of world he'd been safeguarding throughout his career.

His jaw set, Frank paused to listen at the open bay door. Hinges squeaked and voices rose and fell with excitement. An engine whined and he peered around the corner as a forklift with yet another sand-colored container moved up along the pier.

He had to come up with something fast.

Sophia wouldn't wait forever and Halloran's crew probably wouldn't stick around admiring the haul much longer. Frank jogged ahead and waited for the forklift operator to drive by on his way back to the ship.

The machine moved at a good clip, but Frank caught it, hauled himself up and pushed the surprised driver out of the seat. Turning the machine around, he drove straight to Hellfire's warehouse.

Farrell and the men with him saw Frank coming and scattered. A few bullets sparked off the forklift. He kept the machine moving, driving right through the door as they tried to lower it. Metal screeched and groaned. Gunfire erupted, echoing through the warehouse as more bullets ricocheted around the space.

He did as much damage as he could with the forklift, hoping like hell the chaos gave Sophia enough time to pull something useful from the computers. He picked his targets carefully, systematically clearing a path to return to the car. He had to keep them engaged, but if they took him down, Sophia would be trapped. Any second now they'd have men on the roofs with a better firing angle. He had to get her clear before that happened.

A high-pitched scream carried over the

cacophony and froze him in place just outside the warehouse.

The gunfire ceased and a deep voice taunted him, "Give up the fight, Leone."

Frank peeked at the man shouting, saw it was Farrell and quickly decided that was the only good news. Halloran's crew had Sophia surrounded. Farrell had pushed her to her knees, holding her by her hair. Four men fanned out around them, all of them focused on the trashed bay door and the forklift idling noisily.

"Give up," Farrell called out again, "and I'll let her go."

"Don't do it!" Sophia's shout ended in a sputter. Frank's vision hazed red—someone had struck her. He moved silently to a better vantage point, forcing himself to think as a tactician rather than an enraged lover.

She didn't need to worry that he'd believe any promises from Farrell. The man was scum. Taking in the situation, he continued his assessment. Halloran and Hellfire hadn't succeeded because they were sloppy or lazy or left a flank uncovered. They were a brutal team, led by a smart man.

At last Frank spotted the man guarding the path to the front office, and another perched in a makeshift snipers nest in the shelving, covering the men below.

Damn. Even if he had the ammunition, one against seven was long odds. "Way to go, Leone," he muttered under his breath. What had possessed him to let her come along for this one-way ride?

Obviously, he couldn't go straight at them. Farrell or any one of the others—likely all of the others—would riddle him with bullets in an instant, leaving Sophia unprotected. Surrendering was out of the question. Farrell would be sure he and Sophia were sinking to the bottom of the sound within the hour.

While Farrell shouted impotently, Frank crept around, looking for something more effective than his pistol. An airstrike or mortars would be helpful about now. Too bad those were out of his reach. With a start, Frank recognized more numbers and crates. Halloran must be diverting weapons shipments along with the drugs.

Frank quickly found the part numbers he wanted. Quietly, he raised the lid on an open crate and found grenades and a launcher. A bit more firepower than absolutely necessary, but he couldn't help smiling at the potential.

Knowing the guy on the shelves would have the advantage and the best view, Frank took what he needed and shifted to a better strike point. A plan developed as he went along. Take out the guy up top, scatter the others and pick off only enough to ensure Sophia's safe escape.

Much as he wanted to roll a grenade to Farrell's feet, he couldn't risk hitting her or giving them room to take her beyond his reach.

He hefted two types of grenades, his decision made. Making a big enough move to be noticed by the guy nesting in the shelves, he lobbed a smoke grenade in the direction of the office.

The shout from above, along with the pop and smoke, confused Farrell and his men. Frank used those precious seconds to toss an explosive grenade into the steel shelving just under the sniper's perch. Rifle reports sounded and the bullets flew wide when the shooter realized what Frank had done.

The grenade exploded and that end of the warehouse erupted in dust, fire and bits of whatever product might've been stored there. The scream that followed was male this time.

Frank raised his pistol and kneecapped the man closest to the crumpled door. The men flanking Farrell fired, coming closer to hitting Frank's position.

Above the noise of combat, Frank thought he heard Sophia shouting again. He checked, a murderous urge beating in his blood, only to find her armed and Farrell doubled over.

"This way!" he called to her, pinning down Farrell's men with covering fire as she ran to join him. Once she was clear, he pushed her behind him and took the pistol she'd taken from Farrell.

He hefted another smoke grenade and rolled it into the space between them and Farrell's men. They moved closer to the egress, and once Sophia was clear, he pulled the pin and threw another grenade deep into the warehouse. The explosion pushed at the walls as they ran for the safety of the rental car.

Farrell and his men in the warehouse were too busy trying to survive the explosion to give chase. Frank cranked the engine and put the car into Reverse, hurrying away from the compounding destruction as fast as he dared. He wanted to make sure their car wouldn't be caught inside a taped-off crime scene, but he also wanted to be sure the men didn't escape the authorities.

Sirens wailed up and down the pier as police cruisers rolled in and a fireboat churned up the water as it rushed into position.

Frank kept the car running, watching it all unfold from the corner of the parking lot. In the passenger seat, Sophia shivered. Her hands were fisted tight enough to turn the knuckles white.

"We're almost clear." It was the best reassurance he could offer. Everyone was focused on the warehouse. No one cared about a dark blue sedan.

"You did great," she said. "Look, the cops have him now."

Farrell was in cuffs, several of his men behind him. It was a beautiful sight. He turned to kiss Sophia, and his priorities changed when he took a hard look at her. "You're pale. Are you sure you're okay?" Her hands were clamped between her legs and he didn't know what to make of that strange, not-quite-neutral expression on her face.

"I'm fine."

She didn't sound fine. "What happened in the office?" He thought about the scream, the way Farrell had cut her off when she shouted. "Are you hurt?"

"It's not serious."

He put the car in gear and drove away from the pier, aiming for the nearest hospital. "You need an emergency room."

"No, it's not bad, I swear." Her breath hitched. "A rib. That's all. We can't risk an emergency room right now. You're still wanted for murder."

"Who cares? I'm not taking any chances with your health."

"Look at me," she said when he stopped for a traffic light.

He obliged. There were signs of pain in the set of her mouth, the squint of her eyes. "Sophie."

"I'd tell you if I needed a doctor."

"Promise?"

"You can look me over when we get back to the room."

"I'll hold you to that." If he decided she needed medical attention, he wouldn't let her argue.

"Good." She raised a hand and flicked it, indicating he should move along. "I saw an email on the system," she said, her breath catching. "Halloran ordered the warehouse cleaned."

"Guess we helped him out with that explosion." Anything that ultimately helped Halloran maddened Frank, but there hadn't been a choice.

"I don't think we'll get a thank-you note."

His short laugh made her mouth twitch in a semblance of a smile. "Is that all you found?"

"Not even close." She reached under the collar of her shirt and pulled out the flash drive. "Your distraction gave me just enough time.

We'll see what we have when we get back to the room."

And after he checked her ribs. "How did you get out of Farrell's grasp?"

She chuckled and then sucked in a breath at the pain. "He should know better than to put a woman on her knees. His crotch was a prime target. Great job with those grenades."

"Thanks."

"One more thing. I changed the passwords, locking them out of the system and preventing them from wiping any more data."

"Nice."

"I couldn't let you have all the fun," she said.

"Of course not." In all their years, he'd never seen Sophia do anything other than lead by example. Though he'd prefer to spare her any amount of pain and suffering.

He didn't let down his guard until they were back in the hotel room with every available lock engaged.

It worried him a little when she didn't mount much of a protest as he checked her injuries. Her ribs were bruised on the right side, but nothing felt broken. The red welts were already rising and she'd be black-and-blue in the days to come. As she'd said, it wasn't serious, though she needed rest.

He knew better than to suggest it. "We need

supplies to tape your ribs…and something for pain."

"I'll be fine." She gave him a wobbly smile. "Bring me the laptop. You're going to want to see this right away."

The familiar gleam in her eye relaxed him more than anything else. Although she was battered and unhappy about it, her focus hadn't wavered. He helped her get comfortable on the bed, then settled beside her.

Silently, he prayed the risks were about to pay off. He didn't know what he'd do if they couldn't get a net over Halloran and put an end to Hellfire.

Chapter Twelve

Sophia inserted the flash drive into her computer, eager for the relief she knew would flood Frank's face when it all came together. "Getting past the security was easy. They never updated their software and they were too arrogant or neglectful to change the basic admin access codes."

"Was it too easy?"

She turned her face up to look at him, her gaze dropping to his lips for a moment. Kisses should probably wait. "Are you asking if it was a decoy?"

He nodded.

"I don't think so. Take a look." When the files came up, she angled the laptop a bit more for Frank.

He placed his cheaters on his nose and started reading. Those half-glasses shouldn't be a turn-on. He was so sexy, his serious blue eyes taking it all in. In a silly burst of curiosity she wondered if her cheaters had the same effect on him. The man made her want to sigh, though her aching ribs prevented such a response.

He whistled as she pointed out the files she'd managed to grab. Halloran and Farrell had communicated openly with Engle and the crew through emails they considered secure. "Arrogant bastards," Frank muttered.

"As I said, he's ordered inventory cleared out and hard drives wiped. Unfortunately, he can't finish without the new passwords. He can call in someone to help him get back in, but that will take time."

"If we'd waited another day, it would've been too late."

She nodded as he continued to read, his eyes narrowing and his lips flat-lining as the scope of Halloran's treacherous operation started to click. "We have files with monthly reports showing the product and transports. It will take some digging to learn how they diverted the containers."

Frank grunted. "Special Agent Torres suspected Hellfire was behind some of the lost gear."

"The proof is here," she said quietly. "Farrell and Lowry must have won the contract as part of the wink-and-nod system. The contract violations are the least of it." She adjusted the pillow at her back, giving herself a moment as she opened another window. "There was an archived file on Torres, and another on you."

"Kill orders."

She nodded, though it hadn't been a question. "I can't believe Halloran communicated so candidly about the diverted shipments and tweaked manifests, but the murder?"

Frank tugged off his glasses and gave her a weary smile. "Expecting code words and secret handshakes?"

"A girl has her standards," she said, trying to follow his attempt to lighten the mood. They'd survived to this point and, bruised ribs or not, she wasn't giving up yet. "Halloran must already know we were there. When he hears where I was found, he's bound to panic."

"I've been thinking about his exit strategy and options," Frank said, tapping his glasses against his thigh. "He knows his options. He's made a plan."

It took some effort to keep her mind on the data rather than the man beside her while she waited for him to explain.

"How do you suggest we use this?" he asked.

"I'd prefer to send pieces to various places. CID, the reporters and Eddie, too." She hesitated, a little concerned about his reaction. "Because I wasn't sure how much time I had in there, I already forwarded a string of emails to Leo Solutions."

He shifted, dropping his head with a soft thud against the headboard and rubbing his eyes. "Are you using this as leverage against Halloran or me?"

"Oh, stop it." She would not force him into a reunion he wasn't ready for, no matter how eager she was to become a whole family again. "You know me better than that. No one at the office even knows to look for the emails." *Yet.* "I want to contact Halloran and offer to trade this proof of his crimes for our lives." That wouldn't quite restore Frank's reputation, but it was a step in the right direction. "With CID's help we can sort out how he railroaded you."

"Halloran won't go for it." Frank stood and started pacing the room. "He knows I have to throw him under the bus to clear my name."

"We know he's prepared an escape route. The details might be in here."

"If they are, he's moving on to plan B right this minute. At this point, his only chance is to skip the country."

She concentrated on taking slow, careful breaths. "No statute of limitations on murder," she said. "Arranging an exchange for this particular material, evidence he could never shake, is the key. We'll still have plenty to use against him to clear your name. Ideally, we can get a confession out of him."

"Sophie." Frank sighed. "The man isn't a fool."

"No, but we've made him desperate."

"Desperate men do crazy things," he warned. "Let CID take it from here."

"We can do that," she admitted. "Or we can make sure he doesn't slip past them. If we get Leo Solutions involved…" She stopped short at the dark look in her husband's eyes.

"I will not put Frankie in the line of fire," he stated.

She flashed him a look that had made people from several government agencies stop and reconsider. "Find a better argument. Halloran has been using every weapon at his disposal against us, including the press. We have to counter with everything we've got and prove we are the stronger force." The uncertainty in his blue eyes told her he was reconsidering. "If we leave it, that half-baked attempt on the company could be an all-out assault next time," she persisted. "Now is the time to make a stand, and to bring in the heavy artillery."

That earned her a choked laugh. She counted it as progress.

Frank raked his hand through his hair and tugged at the roots. She sympathized with his frustration. Halloran had played a nasty game and they were so close to stealing a win.

"I won't allow you to push us away again."

"Sophia." He sighed, his eyes so sad. "They nearly killed you a few hours ago."

She pulled the clip out of her hair, shaking it loose, an effective distraction for him. When his gaze warmed, it melted the last of the persistent chill in her veins from the near miss. "They didn't succeed. All thanks to you."

He turned his back to her and she realized how close she was to losing everything. Again. How many times could a woman pick herself up from a pit of despair? If he went after Halloran alone, thinking to protect her and Frankie, the odds of restoring his reputation and life were slim to none. If he walked away in some misplaced gesture of honor, it would break her. She refused to give him the option.

She ignored the discomfort and slid out of the bed. The short carpet was rough under her bare feet. She moved up behind him. His muscles felt warm and strong beneath her palms when she pressed her hands to his shoulders. She dug her thumbs into the tension at his neck. "You know that bringing in Frankie, Aidan and whoever else we need at the company is the right tactic," she murmured quietly, letting the words drift over him.

"She's…" His voice trailed off.

"She's not a child," Sophia reminded him. "She *is* a warrior, Frank—you know that." She swallowed back the urgency, the desperation. She couldn't give Frank any reason to dismiss her idea too quickly. "We have to look at our daughter as a peer in this case, not as our baby." She kept up her massage as she shared her idea. "There is one man left."

"One man with who knows how much support."

She ignored that for the moment. "We have Frankie, Aidan and the assets of our company."

"Your company."

She ignored that, too. When this was over, they could argue ownership versus partnership. "The point is we have backup. Let's use it, throw everything we've got at him. Halloran and Hellfire will crumble under the barrage."

He reached up and trapped one of her hands at his shoulder. "You won't take no for an answer, will you?"

"Would you, in my place?"

"No." He took a deep breath, let it out slowly. "I've never stopped loving you," he said quietly.

"I know." While she hadn't appreciated his

distance or extreme methods, in his shoes she would have done whatever seemed necessary to protect the family. That was what she was doing right now, in fact. The challenges and pressures of his career and hers had reinforced their independence even as they'd been forged into a team. Through different means and skills, both of them had a deep, intrinsic need to protect and defend. Had there ever been two people better suited?

"I love you, too." She hoped the depth of love rekindled through this crisis would make them stronger—strong enough to stick together through the rest of their lives. First they had to survive this. If even one of the bastards slipped free, they'd forever be leery of another attack. She wouldn't allow that kind of trouble to hover over her family's horizon.

He turned around, cradling her face and kissing her with devastating tenderness. Relief and hope washed over her in a sweet wave. Her lips moved against his, giving back every precious touch and affirmation that they would get through this together.

Frank eased back, his hands gentle on her arms. "I don't want to see Frankie until Halloran's in custody. Not until it's all over."

"Why not?" She thought she knew, but better to hear it from him, to make him state his reasons aloud.

He took a sudden interest in the ceiling. "I can't," he whispered. "I don't want her to see me when there's a cloud hanging over my head."

She felt for her husband. Frank had shouldered the weight of a bad situation and blamed himself for the actions of a few bad men. "She never stopped believing you were a hero," she reminded him, though it wouldn't change his mind.

He said nothing.

"Let's work out the details of tempting Halloran," she offered, "and then we can decide who else we'll need from the company." Getting him back into analysis mode was essential to wrap this up.

He nodded, his mind working on the tactical problem again. "The money isn't enough of a lure. The password lockout might not be enough." He sighed. "How do we convince him we haven't already passed the murder evidence up the line?"

She loved watching her husband think. Or pace, or simply sleep, she admitted, yanking her mind back on point. "What if we make it personal?"

"It's never been anything but personal. These are proud men, Sophia."

"I know the type," she muttered.

"The stakes in Hellfire were clear from the start," he continued. "Failure carries the death penalty. Everyone involved created places to hide in countries that don't cooperate with United States extradition orders. Much as we can't stop until we catch them, they can't leave anyone alive who knows their secrets."

She'd suspected this from the beginning, watching the ax swing ever closer to Frank's head. Hearing the brutal facts stated so simply in his resounding baritone threw her heart rate into high gear. "We need a confession," she insisted. "We'll be the bait. You and me. We can offer him the evidence if he lets us be. We'll choose the place and Leo Solutions can watch our backs." It was the only option left, Frank had to know that.

"They'll anticipate the move," he argued.

"I know. We'll give them what they expect to see."

"Which is?"

She swallowed the ball of nerves lodged in her throat. "A scared wife and mother begging for mercy."

Frank snorted. "He'll never buy into that. He knows you, remember?"

She'd preen over that compliment later. "Well, maybe a variation on that theme." She returned to the bed and her laptop to draft the email that would hopefully bring Halloran close enough to catch.

They worked and debated every word until Frank was sure they had the hook in deep. They set the meet for tomorrow on the first ferry from Seattle to Victoria, British Columbia.

"What next?" Frank asked as she booked the ferry tickets online.

"As connected as Halloran's spies have been all along, I think it's only fair we let him think he's got us. I'll ask for what I need from Leo Solutions in a way that looks benign to Hellfire in case that hack left them some access the company hasn't spotted yet." She started typing her email, fine-tuning that as well before she filled in the recipient address. She glanced at Frank. "Thoughts?"

His eyes widened, his salt-and-pepper eyebrows arching as the scope of her suggestion took shape. "A spin on the classic headache ploy."

"Yes." When Frankie had started going out on her own to parties and on dates, they'd taught her she only had to call home, claim she had a headache and Sophia or Frank would come get her, no questions asked.

"You're sure Frankie will understand what amounts to a coded message?"

"Absolutely." A few months ago her daughter had been avoiding every attempt at contact or reconciliation. Now Sophia enjoyed a close relationship with Frankie again as if no time had passed. It would help that she'd kept Aidan updated through a private channel since she'd left the hotel in Chicago. She didn't see the wisdom in revealing that to Frank just yet. The plan gave him enough to chew on as it was. If everything worked, he'd be reunited with his daughter before the three-hour ferry trip was over.

As long as no one died.

Chapter Thirteen

Saturday, April 23, 7:00 a.m.

"I don't like it."

Frank looked out over the water as they waited in line to board the ferry. His wife would be bait. He could practically see the blood staining his hands. His daughter and her fiancé were supposedly close, though he hadn't spotted her. "Three hours on a boat with Halloran and his men." He wanted to cover Sophia in body armor and send her far from here. This was a bad idea. "Too much can go wrong."

Sophia linked her arm through his as their boarding group time was called. "We need the confession to wrap this up," she reminded him gently.

His wife wore a wire a tech from Leo Solutions had dropped off at the hotel last night. She had a script memorized so she could chat up the monster trying to flee the country. It wasn't right. To his eternal frustration, Frank knew he'd only lose the argument again if he advocated for tossing Halloran overboard.

"You're entitled to reclaim your life," she added. "More than that."

What did that mean? He focused on the current crisis rather than the questions about their future. "It will be at least three against two with all these civilians caught in between."

"You're right," she said. "He doesn't stand a chance." She tipped up her face and gave him a razor-sharp smile.

That look, that sheer determination and faith in what they were about to do, anchored him, reestablishing his focus. Thankfully, he didn't have more time to question the plan. All around them people boarded the ferry, several families chattering with excitement about the trip ahead and the whales they might see along the way. It was painfully normal.

Frank bent his lips to her ear. "I won't let him hurt you." Never again.

"Same goes," she whispered, her smile softening. "Let's finish this."

His stomach twisted a little tighter. Failure wasn't an option. His daughter needed her mother. If only one of them could get back to Seattle, Frank was determined it would be Sophia. His daughter had learned to live without her father once. He wouldn't let Halloran rob Frankie of her mother, too.

Frank and Sophia walked together along the ferry, pausing periodically at the rails as though they were tourists heading off for a weekend getaway. Neither of them had spotted Halloran yet, though Frank recognized one man from yesterday's attack on the warehouse and assumed the grim-looking man with him was also a Hellfire spy. The men were sticking a little too close to the stairs to the upper deck.

"They've made us."

"Naturally." Sophia was so cool it unnerved him. "Relax. I doubt he'll even approach me until we're under way."

"You can't go to him," Frank insisted. "I won't let you be alone with him."

"Frank." Her voice was stone-cold, in direct contrast to the soft smile on her face. How did she do that? "I'm a general's wife—your wife. He'll come to me."

Frank glanced around the deck. It was a beautiful day with soft morning sunlight filling a blue sky and glazing the water. If they got the confession, he might just enjoy the trip back. "Something's not right."

"That's enough," Sophia scolded. "I'll toss

you overboard and handle this myself if you don't pull yourself together."

The image of his wife doing just that made him laugh. "God, you're incredible."

"I know it." Her smile was sincere and warm this time. "He'll come to me, Frank, because we have what he needs to get away cleanly."

He knew she was right. Taking a deep breath, he draped his arm across her shoulder and resigned himself to letting the operation play out. "Remember our first time on this ferry?" They'd come to Seattle to check out the quarters in anticipation of their move to his last duty station. It had been a whirlwind trip of sightseeing, exploring the area and talking about what they might do with retirement.

Her cheeks turned rosy. "I was recalling our second water excursion."

"If I spend any time thinking about that, I might not care if Halloran gets away." That had been a private, guided cruise around the nearby islands. After a stunning sunset, they'd retreated to the cabin and made love the whole way back to Seattle.

As the ferry eased away from the Seattle terminal, she leaned back into the rail, pulling her sunglasses down so he could see her eyes. "Want to know a secret?"

"Always." No matter how much time together or apart, he loved discovering and rediscovering every nuance and detail about his wife.

"I'm hoping one day soon you and I will resume our exploration of the many islands and waterways around here."

His heart hammered at the hot, blatant invitation in her eyes. There was no mistaking her intent. She wanted him to stay if they managed to succeed. He had opened his mouth to say the words, to leave no room for her to doubt how much he wanted to spend every remaining day of his life with her, when he spotted their target.

"Halloran."

She reached up and laid her warm palm on his cheek. "Here we go."

He inhaled her words, willed them to be true. At least three against two and she obviously *believed* they held the advantage.

What did he know? She'd been right about everything else and planned for every contingency. Thanks to Leo Solutions, they had the best recording device available. They knew what Halloran could and couldn't do to disable it. With a bit of luck, this long nightmare would be over soon. Frank had spent enough of his life apart from the people who mattered most. It was high time the right man faced justice.

Sophia squeezed his fingers and moved toward the stern, the place Halloran had designated for the exchange in his confirmation email. When the bastard accepted that flash drive, it would be over.

Provided his men didn't kill Frank and Sophia in the process. As Sophia walked toward the meet with Halloran, Frank strolled aft to intercept the man he'd recognized earlier. With a cluster of tourists between them, Frank knelt to tie his shoe. When he stood, his ball cap was a different color and he'd pulled off his dark windbreaker, tying it around his waist.

It gave him room to work and he used those few seconds to his advantage. Getting behind Halloran's man, Frank heard him admit he'd lost visual. Almost immediately his counterpart changed direction and hurried to the upper level.

He waited until a family with excited children hurried down the stairs, using them as a distraction. Cautiously, he moved along the upper deck, searching for Halloran's other spy. He caught sight of him near the crates of checked baggage. Knowing Halloran was planning to escape the country, what had he brought along that warranted two guards?

Ducking out of sight, he slipped his jacket back on, one more layer of defense if this turned into a fight. He assessed his potential opponent. Young and tall, the spy would surely have been warned about Frank's skills.

Frank boldly approached. "Nice view up here. Too bad your boss is missing it."

"He probably prefers sharing the scenery with your wife." The spy stood loose and light on his feet, clearly eager for a physical conflict. It was a good thing Sophia had refused to let Frank carry any weapons today, he thought. He'd happily kneecap this guy and consider it a public service.

Frank raised his chin to the locked baggage crates. "What does he think you can success-fully protect?"

"Everything." It had to be drugs or cash for a bribe at the border.

"Let's test that theory." Frank stepped in close and stomped his boot hard on the spy's foot. The man groaned and Frank drove his knee up into his belly. Amid gasps and curses, Frank swiftly struck and retreated until the younger man crumpled. No weapon required.

As he patted down the stunned spy, he found a belt wallet with a bit of heft and a small re-volver in an ankle holster. Frank pocketed both for later analysis and took the spy's earpiece, as well.

One down, one to go.

As the ferry churned along, Frank found a vacated seat in the center section, waiting for the second spy to come up the stairs any minute. It was a struggle not to break the plan and go check on his wife. He forced himself to stay put. His task was to keep Halloran's thugs busy and the playing field even. He drummed his fingers on the belt wallet, listening and waiting.

The second spy didn't come upstairs and he didn't check in. The lack of communication alarmed Frank. Taking a minute, he unzipped the wallet and found a small fortune in uncut rubies. He felt like an idiot for not anticipating another wrinkle. Halloran had his hands deep into every possible pie.

Untraceable, gemstones were easier to hide and to liquidate than laundering vast amounts of US currency. For a man on the run, rubies could very well get Halloran out of the country. "Not today," Frank murmured to himself.

Plan or not, with no concern from the second spy, Frank couldn't waste another minute. Even with Leo Solutions' support and technology, Sophia needed him watching her back personally.

NEAR THE STERN with the wake of the high-speed ferry streaming white behind them,

Sophia watched Seattle drift farther into the distance. She'd lost sight of Frank, which didn't worry her, because Halloran and one of his men were with her. Frank could hold his own one-on-one with anyone.

She had yet to get Halloran to admit or agree to anything. She worried it wouldn't happen at all. The retired general would rightly assume she was wired and would be trying to jam that signal. He couldn't know about the video feed Aidan and Frankie had managed to get installed on the ferry last night—unless he'd bribed someone else to keep watch. As confident as she'd been for her husband, she was starting to have doubts about success.

"Just tell me why," she suggested, not for the first time. "We were friends once. You owe me that much at least."

"It was business," Halloran said, his voice cold. "You and Frank were merely casualties of an operational success."

"Cut the crap." Throwing him overboard was sounding better. "You railroaded my husband for what? A few thousand dollars."

He laughed. "I know you've looked into the accounts."

She shrugged. "I didn't find anything that would stick. I'll hand over everything, Kelly. Just tell me why you chose Frank as the patsy."

"Hellfire had a stiff admission price," Halloran said. "You'll notice the price for betrayal was higher still." He held out his hand. "Give me the drive."

She didn't take her eyes off his weathered face. It made her sick to think how he was touted as a hero, yet he'd sacrificed innocent lives for the sake of lining his pockets with gold. "You haven't given me any assurance that my family will be safe."

Another humorless laugh made her cringe. "You were one of the rare gems," he said. "Frank was lucky to have you."

Her eyes darted around the deck at the use of the past tense. "He *is* lucky to have me," she corrected. "Give me some sign of good faith that if I hand this over you'll leave us alone," she repeated.

"What's better than my word?" he asked. "You can't expect me to put it in writing."

She affected a sigh, as if he'd outmaneuvered her. "You know I'm wired."

"Of course I know," he said with a slimy smile. "You're no fool. How else would you prove you haven't been cooperating with me all along?"

Halloran's smug expression made her queasy. She supposed, if she let that sick feeling show on her face, he'd think he had her.

"Lawyers and investigators picked through my life when Frank was on trial. They know I wasn't complicit."

She had to get Halloran to admit to something, preferably the treason or the murder. She pulled the mic and wire from beneath the collar of her sweater, showing him it was disconnected, and dropped it into his open palm. "Why, Kelly? Between you and me and the disabled wire, tell me why."

"Calling a stalemate, huh?"

She nodded. "You'll disappear, Frank will be haunted by false charges and I'll forever be waiting for you to strike again." She held up her hands in surrender, though she was doing nothing of the kind. "You win."

"Give me the drive." For the first time, his voice resembled the man who'd been her friend.

She handed it over, praying the closed-circuit system and the secondary mic running on a different frequency were working properly.

He signaled his spy to come closer. The man inserted the flash drive into a tablet. After a moment he gave his boss a nod that the contents were genuine and moved out of earshot again. "Thank you." Halloran's face twisted into a sneer; evidently he believed he had the only remaining evidence she'd gathered against him, along with the new passwords giving him access to his system again. "It was business," he repeated. "With a little personal," he said slowly. "I couldn't believe he turned on me. He saw the numbers, the potential. Through Hellfire, he could've given you a limitless future."

"With blood money."

"The whole world runs on blood money," Halloran said, flinging out a hand. "We made this bed we're stuck in, manipulating this leader for that resource. I did terrible things in the name of your freedom. My pet project wasn't anything different than what the government has done. What made me a criminal was doing it for personal gain."

"You actually believe that." She kept an eye out for Frank, eager to give him the takedown signal.

"I've lived it," Halloran was saying. "Frank's lived it. That's what made him such a great fit."

"Kelly, you can't really believe that."

"Don't take that tone with me." He snatched her elbow in a hard grip and forced her to look out to sea, away from any passengers. "A report doesn't convey with any accuracy the things we've seen and done in the field. I did plenty of good out there and then I took control. Made things even better. Only God will tell me if I went too far."

Sophia felt more than qualified to tell him he'd gone too far, but it would fall on deaf ears and an empty conscience.

"You have what you need. Take your hands off my wife."

At the sound of Frank's voice, Sophia nearly cheered.

"I'll do whatever I please," Halloran said, twisting around and using Sophia as a shield.

"Keep that up," Frank said to him. "Give me a reason to do what I so desperately want to do. Right now. Right here."

Furious at Halloran's pointless actions, Sophia didn't bother to struggle. There wasn't much he could do here on a crowded ferry. Had he overlooked the two hundred witnesses milling around?

"Let my wife go." Frank took a menacing step closer. "Or you can take a swim right now."

"Your hands are as tied as mine, General Leone!" Halloran shouted the name. Faces turned their way with varying degrees of concern and irritation. "I control all of it now." He shoved Sophia hard, the deck railing biting into her bruised ribs. Frank took a step, and Halloran whipped out a knife and pressed it to her throat.

"Stay back," Halloran yelled.

People around them gasped and moved back. Some pulled out phones and started recording, while others urged children to a safer distance. Sophia wanted to laugh. Knives were a respected weapon but hardly a challenge to the Leone family. Frank had given countless young soldiers classes on knife combat and defense.

"This is ridiculous, Kelly," she said. The man was coming unhinged. "You have everything you demanded."

The ferry's minimal security team was already approaching. There was nowhere for Halloran to run.

She exchanged a look with Frank, hoping he understood and trusted her judgment. "What was the plan, Kelly? Take the evidence and bribe your way across the border?"

Frank nodded his support of her tactic. "Uncut rubies," Frank answered, holding up the belt wallet.

"Give that to me!" Halloran couldn't hold her and take the rubies. Something had to give.

Taking advantage of his indecision, Sophia plowed an elbow into his ribs as she pushed away the knife with her free hand. The second she was clear, Frank lunged, slamming Halloran hard on the deck. Security closed around them. Focused on Halloran, the security team didn't see Halloran's spy draw his gun and take aim at Frank.

Sophia shoved Frank, knocking him into one of the security guards. As the men stumbled and scrambled, the spy fired. The bullet missed Frank and hit Halloran in the chest. Sophia rushed to the man who'd put them all through hell, determined to keep him alive long enough to clear Frank's name.

Time blurred as paramedics arrived, nudging her into Frank's solid embrace. The ferry reached the island and slowly the passengers were cleared one by one to disembark. Halloran and his last two loyal spies were taken into custody and ushered back to Seattle by a hydrofoil.

Through the combined support of Sophia's connections, the Colby Agency and Aidan's international contacts, she and Frank were transported by helicopter to Joint Base Lewis-McChord, where an army CID special agent took their statements. When the formalities were completed, the special agent confirmed Engle, Lowry and Farrell would all remain in federal custody, along with their associates.

By nightfall, Frank was declared officially alive and cleared to go home, no longer a murder suspect. In the coming days, his service record would be set straight and he would be absolved of any and all crimes. Though they were asked to remain in the country until the paperwork was complete, the special agent addressed him by his proper rank and ordered an official car to take them home.

"Home," he mused, his voice full of wonder, as they stood side by side waiting for the car. "I'd almost given up on the idea."

It had started to rain and Sophia wanted nothing more than to be at peace with her husband watching that rain from the little bistro table on her front porch. "Come home with me," she said. "At least for tonight."

"Sophie…"

"What is it?"

"Did you hear from Frankie? Was she there today? Too ashamed to speak to me?"

Sophia smiled up at him. "She wasn't there. Knowing your wishes, Aidan and I had other people onboard for any needed backup."

He rubbed his eyes and swallowed hard. "Thank you."

Her heart ached for everything he'd endured. "Come home with me, Frank. We've had enough hotels for a while. I think you'll like what I did with the house." She'd asked Frankie and Aidan to wait for them there. "There's a perfectly tidy guest room if—"

He moved so swiftly she lost her breath as

he kissed her soundly. "I won't sleep if I'm apart from you."

The earnestness in his blue eyes melted her heart.

The car arrived and she took his hand when he seemed frozen by uncertainty. "Then come home, Frank. It's past time."

FRANK KNEW SHE was up to something. She had that look in her eye, the same look he'd seen on his fortieth birthday when she'd surprised him with a party at the office. He didn't deserve a party tonight. Not after he'd shut out the two people who meant the most to him in this world. He wasn't sure he deserved to stick around, to maintain any sort of contact.

His choices had hurt all three of them. Would they truly be able to overcome it?

"I should stay at a hotel," he murmured, terrified he knew exactly what Sophia was up to. The idea of seeing his daughter again scared him more than Halloran's potential escape. How could he face Frankie? How could he ask for her forgiveness for all he'd put her through? "I wouldn't know where to start explaining to her."

He watched the rain-soaked streets flash by under the streetlamps.

Sophia's hand slipped into his. "You knew well enough where to start with me."

"That was different."

"Why?"

He couldn't articulate it, couldn't push the words past the lump in his throat. "Maybe after the wedding. I shouldn't intrude."

"Oh, what a ridiculous thing to say." Her fingers dug into his a little too hard. "And selfish."

He turned away from the gloomy view. "Selfish? I'm trying to do the right thing here." He attempted to tug his hand free, but she wouldn't let go.

"Then do the right thing."

He was surprised to see no judgment in her deep brown eyes, only peace, affection and an underlying understanding.

"She loves you," Sophia said. "Planning the wedding has been a delicate balancing act because she's so happy with Aidan and so sad you're not around."

"She can't possibly still need me. You've told me repeatedly how capable and independent she is."

The car turned into Queen Anne, and he felt his heart rate speed up, knowing the moment of truth was nearly upon him.

"Frank," she urged gently, "no matter how

independent or capable, a girl always needs her father." She raised his hand to her face and rubbed it against her soft cheek. "If you bail now, you'll do irrevocable damage."

His wife's assessment scared him. Was it selfish to want to put this off another day?

"She understands mission and classified information," Sophia continued. "Trust her. Trust me."

"I do." He trusted her more than he'd ever trusted anyone. Loved his girls. "I love you. Both of you."

"We know."

"The idea of hurting you, of adding to the damage I've already done…" He ran out of words again.

Sophia shifted closer, her thigh rubbing along his. "You did what was necessary. Do you honestly think we'd fault you for it?"

"*Dolcezza*, you're too good for me." The car stopped on a neighborhood street and he looked around. "Queen Anne?"

"Just as we planned," she said, her eyes bright.

"I was convicted of treason," he said, stunned. "Why hang on to our dream?"

"I suppose it was my way of hanging on to you, my love. Come inside and let's be a family again."

Before he could protest or beg for more time, the front door flew open and Frankie raced down the steps, heedless of the wet weather. She nearly careened into the sedan in her haste to wrench open the door.

"Daddy!"

Frank climbed out and found himself tugged into his daughter's embrace as the soft night rain washed away the last of his guilt and trepidation. He held her tight in his arms and Sophia joined them in a group hug.

The nightmare was truly over. He was home and nothing would tear him away again.

Chapter Fourteen

Saturday, September 27, 6:30 p.m.

Frank's heart pounded as he waited for his daughter to join him at the back door of the lovely estate where she would exchange vows with Aidan in the garden in mere minutes. He'd thought this day out of his reach. To be reunited with his family, to feel whole inside and out—well, the reality of it was still sinking in.

He'd never been happier, except on the day he'd exchanged vows with his remarkable wife, Sophia.

Frankie peeked around the corner, then rushed forward, a glowing vision in her mother's redesigned wedding gown. She lifted her veil to kiss his cheek, bouncing a little on her toes. "You're radiant," he whispered, kissing her cheek in turn. A stronger voice was out of his reach. "Aidan will be speechless."

"Not too speechless, I hope," Frankie said, her eyes sparkling with absolute joy. "He has some important words to say." Her gaze dropped to the bouquet in her hands before she raised those warm brown eyes, so like her mother's, to his once more. "I'm so thankful you're here, Daddy. This day wouldn't have been the same without you."

He placed her hand on his arm when the music changed for her entrance. They heard the rustle of movement as guests got to their feet. "Thanks for your faith in me, sunshine."

She took a deep breath and gave his arm a little squeeze. "Let's go before they send out a search party."

They started down the aisle, as stately as they'd rehearsed, each step taking him closer to the moment when he would give away his daughter, his only child, to the man of her dreams. He knew his first look should've been to double-check the groom's reaction, to be sure the young man was up to the task to love, honor and cherish Frank's baby. Instead, his gaze landed on his wife, the woman who had embodied all his dreams from the first moment he'd laid eyes on her over three decades ago.

Somehow he managed to give his daughter to her groom and take his seat beside Sophia without tripping over his lines or his feet. He had to assume the ceremony was perfect, as the moment overwhelmed him and he didn't hear much of it. Thank goodness, there would be video. In what felt like a matter of seconds, the minister pronounced Frankie and Aidan married.

As the guests were ushered toward the reception, Frank couldn't stop smiling as the families were posed this way and that for official pictures. At last they were done and heading back up the lawns to join the reception in the estate ballroom.

Sophia slipped her hand into his. "Congratulations, darling. We did it."

He wasn't sure if she referred to the dangers they'd survived or reaching this milestone as parents. Not that it mattered. They were together and they'd get to enjoy the next stage of their lives together. Just as they had planned.

Still, he felt as if the moment needed a bigger gesture, some way to symbolize his return to the man she trusted with her heart and her future.

Sophia stroked her free hand over their joined hands. "Will you walk with me a minute?"

He smiled. "You should know by now that I'd walk with you anywhere."

She smiled back. "To hell and back maybe?" she queried. "Yes, I noticed."

To Frank's surprise, Sophia led him to a quiet, meditation garden. At the far end a waterfall trickled merrily down over a clever tumble of rocks. Flowers spilled over the edges of big planters, and benches flanked a reflecting pool in the center.

As if on cue, the minister stepped in front of the waterfall, Victoria and Lucas in his wake.

"I'd marry you all over again, Franklin Leone. I thought it would be a nice gesture if we renewed our vows."

Nice? He thought it would be perfect. "I'd be honored, *dolcezza*."

She twisted off the wedding rings she'd just started wearing again and put them in his palm. He gave his ring to her and they stepped forward.

Frank's voice was strong as he spoke his vows, as strong as the spirit of the woman who'd loved him through thirty years of better and worse already. When she gave him her vows and slid that band of gold back into place on his finger, his heart soared.

"I love you," he said, his hands at her waist. "You're stuck with me forever now."

"For at least thirty more years," she said, wrapping her arms around his neck. "I love you."

The kiss was interrupted by a happy cheer and the pop of a champagne cork as Frankie and Aidan surprised them. Frank planted another kiss on Sophia's sweet lips. Then, amid delighted laughter, he opened his arms wide for a family hug and a private toast to the most important people in his life.

VICTORIA DABBED AT her eyes with the handkerchief Lucas had given her. Her husband wrapped her arm around his. "How lucky we are to have witnessed a miracle," Lucas said gently.

She smiled up at him. "We've witnessed a few in our time."

Lucas stopped a waiter and claimed two glasses of champagne. He offered one to her and then tapped his glass to hers. "To many more, my dear."

Victoria savored the bubbly taste and smiled. "Many more, indeed."

* * * * *

Don't miss the first in the brand-new
FACES OF EVIL: PRIVATE EYES *series*
coming from Debra Webb and
Harlequin Intrigue in September 2016!
Look for the first brand-new adventure
from Regan Black and
Harlequin Romantic Suspense
in November 2016!

LARGER-PRINT BOOKS!

HARLEQUIN

Presents®

GET 2 FREE LARGER-PRINT NOVELS PLUS 2 FREE GIFTS!

PASSION GUARANTEED SEDUCTION

YES! Please send me 2 FREE LARGER-PRINT Harlequin Presents® novels and my 2 FREE gifts (gifts are worth about $10). After receiving them, if I don't wish to receive any more books, I can return the shipping statement marked "cancel." If I don't cancel, I will receive 6 brand-new novels every month and be billed just $5.30 per book in the U.S. or $5.74 per book in Canada. That's a saving of at least 12% off the cover price! It's quite a bargain! Shipping and handling is just 50¢ per book in the U.S. and 75¢ per book in Canada.* I understand that accepting the 2 free books and gifts places me under no obligation to buy anything. I can always return a shipment and cancel at any time. Even if I never buy another book, the two free books and gifts are mine to keep forever.

176/376 HDN GHVY

Name	(PLEASE PRINT)

Address		Apt. #

City	State/Prov.	Zip/Postal Code

Signature (if under 18, a parent or guardian must sign)

Mail to the **Reader Service:**
IN U.S.A.: P.O. Box 1867, Buffalo, NY 14240-1867
IN CANADA: P.O. Box 609, Fort Erie, Ontario L2A 5X3

**Are you a subscriber to Harlequin Presents® books
and want to receive the larger-print edition?
Call 1-800-873-8635 today or visit us at www.ReaderService.com.**

* Terms and prices subject to change without notice. Prices do not include applicable taxes. Sales tax applicable in N.Y. Canadian residents will be charged applicable taxes. Offer not valid in Quebec. This offer is limited to one order per household. Not valid for current subscribers to Harlequin Presents Larger-Print books. All orders subject to credit approval. Credit or debit balances in a customer's account(s) may be offset by any other outstanding balance owed by or to the customer. Please allow 4 to 6 weeks for delivery. Offer available while quantities last.

Your Privacy—The Reader Service is committed to protecting your privacy. Our Privacy Policy is available online at www.ReaderService.com or upon request from the Reader Service.

We make a portion of our mailing list available to reputable third parties that offer products we believe may interest you. If you prefer that we not exchange your name with third parties, or if you wish to clarify or modify your communication preferences, please visit us at www.ReaderService.com/consumerschoice or write to us at Reader Service Preference Service, P.O. Box 9062, Buffalo, NY 14240-9062. Include your complete name and address.

HPLP15

LARGER-PRINT BOOKS!
GET 2 FREE LARGER-PRINT NOVELS PLUS
2 FREE GIFTS!

HARLEQUIN®

Romance

From the Heart, For the Heart

LARGER-PRINT BOOKS!
GET 2 FREE LARGER-PRINT NOVELS PLUS
2 FREE GIFTS!

HARLEQUIN

super romance

More Story...More Romance

YES! Please send me 2 FREE LARGER-PRINT Harlequin® Superromance® novels and my 2 FREE gifts (gifts are worth about $10). After receiving them, if I don't wish to receive any more books, I can return the shipping statement marked "cancel." If I don't cancel, I will receive 4 brand-new novels every month and be billed just $5.94 per book in the U.S. or $6.24 per book in Canada. That's a savings of at least 12% off the cover price! It's quite a bargain! Shipping and handling is just 50¢ per book in the U.S. or 75¢ per book in Canada.* I understand that accepting the 2 free books and gifts places me under no obligation to buy anything. I can always return a shipment and cancel at any time. Even if I never buy another book, the two free books and gifts are mine to keep forever.

132/332 HDN GHVC

Name _____ (PLEASE PRINT) _____

Address _____ Apt. # _____

City _____ State/Prov. _____ Zip/Postal Code _____

Signature (if under 18, a parent or guardian must sign)

Mail to the **Reader Service:**
IN U.S.A.: P.O. Box 1867, Buffalo, NY 14240-1867
IN CANADA: P.O. Box 609, Fort Erie, Ontario L2A 5X3

Want to try two free books from another line?
Call 1-800-873-8635 today or visit www.ReaderService.com.

* Terms and prices subject to change without notice. Prices do not include applicable taxes. Sales tax applicable in N.Y. Canadian residents will be charged applicable taxes. Offer not valid in Quebec. This offer is limited to one order per household. Not valid for current subscribers to Harlequin Superromance Larger-Print books. All orders subject to credit approval. Credit or debit balances in a customer's account(s) may be offset by any other outstanding balance owed by or to the customer. Please allow 4 to 6 weeks for delivery. Offer available while quantities last.

Your Privacy—The Reader Service is committed to protecting your privacy. Our Privacy Policy is available online at www.ReaderService.com or upon request from the Reader Service.

We make a portion of our mailing list available to reputable third parties that offer products we believe may interest you. If you prefer that we not exchange your name with third parties, or if you wish to clarify or modify your communication preferences, please visit us at www.ReaderService.com/consumerchoice or write to us at Reader Service Preference Service, P.O. Box 9062, Buffalo, NY 14240-9062. Include your complete name and address.

HSRLP15

YES! Please send me **The Montana Mavericks Collection** in Larger Print. This collection begins with 3 FREE books and 2 FREE gifts (gifts valued at approx. $20.00 retail) in the first shipment, along with the other first 4 books from the collection! If I do not cancel, I will receive 8 monthly shipments until I have the entire 51-book Montana Mavericks collection. I will receive 2 or 3 FREE books in each shipment and I will pay just $4.99 US/ $5.89 CDN for each of the other four books in each shipment, plus $2.99 for shipping and handling per shipment.*If I decide to keep the entire collection, I'll have paid for only 32 books, because 19 books are FREE! I understand that accepting the 3 free books and gifts places me under no obligation to buy anything. I can always return a shipment and cancel at any time. My free books and gifts are mine to keep no matter what I decide.

263 HCN 2404   463 HCN 2404

Name	(PLEASE PRINT)	
Address		Apt. #
City	State/Prov.	Zip/Postal Code

Signature (if under 18, a parent or guardian must sign)

Mail to the **Reader Service:**

IN U.S.A.: P.O. Box 1867, Buffalo, NY 14240-1867
IN CANADA: P.O. Box 609, Fort Erie, Ontario L2A 5X3